"I'm Prepa[red To Cancel] The Debt You Owe Me, If You Give Me A Child."

Piper gasped. "You're talking about a baby! Not some pawn in a game of chess."

"You're in a position to repay me?" Wade asked.

"You know damn well that I can't pay you back."

When his hands settled on her shoulders she flinched, but it didn't deter him. Instead he turned her body and enveloped her in his arms. It shouldn't feel so good. She should pull away, refuse his offer of solace—he was the enemy—but instead, she welcomed his embrace.

"Would it be so bad, Piper? We were good together once."

"Please," she said, her voice strained and small. "Give me time to work something out."

"You have until dinner tonight."

* * *

Dear Reader,

I'm frequently asked by readers, and sometimes just those who are curious, where I get my ideas. It often makes me pause and wonder, too. ☺

Essentially, my story ideas evolve from a trigger. That trigger can be a snippet I might hear on the news or a line from a song's lyrics, or even a picture of a house. Once that trigger does its stuff, my mind is stimulated to twist and turn the snippet, or the line from the song, into a gazillion "what if" scenarios. The same, too, with a picture of a house. What kind of people live there? How long has this house been a part of them? Is it even a part of them and, if not, why not?

With *The Pregnancy Contract,* there were various triggers and one of the key ones is a very lovely historical home, called Alberton, in the city where I live. I haven't visited the house recently, but the memory of previous visits always lingers inside me. And with those memories, the very strong impression that it was very much a 'family' home. So then I started to wonder— what if someone had taken for granted that this family home would always be there, always be theirs? What if, one day, they came home and it wasn't?

I hope you enjoy *The Pregnancy Contract.* It was a very emotional story to write and one that made me sigh with satisfaction when Piper and Wade finally reached their happy-ever-after.

Happy reading!

Yvonne Lindsay

YVONNE LINDSAY

THE PREGNANCY CONTRACT

Recycling programs
for this product may
not exist in your area.

ISBN-13: 978-0-373-73130-5

THE PREGNANCY CONTRACT

Recent books by Yvonne Lindsay

Harlequin Desire

Bought: His Temporary Fiancée #2078
The Pregnancy Contract #2117

Silhouette Desire

*The Boss's Christmas Seduction #1758
*The CEO's Contract Bride #1776
*The Tycoon's Hidden Heir #1788
Rossellini's Revenge Affair #1811
Tycoon's Valentine Vendetta #1854
Jealousy & A Jewelled Proposition #1873
Claiming His Runaway Bride #1890
†Convenient Marriage, Inconvenient Husband #1923
†Secret Baby, Public Affair #1930
†Pretend Mistress, Bona Fide Boss #1937
Defiant Mistress, Ruthless Millionaire #1986
**Honor-Bound Groom #2029
**Stand-In Bride's Seduction #2038
**For the Sake of the Secret Child #2044

*New Zealand Knights
†Rogue Diamonds
**Wed at Any Price

All backlist available in ebook

YVONNE LINDSAY

New Zealand born, to Dutch immigrant parents, Yvonne Lindsay became an avid romance reader at the age of thirteen. Now, married to her 'blind date' and with two fabulous children, she remains a firm believer in the power of romance. Yvonne feels privileged to be able to bring to her readers the stories of her heart. In her spare time, when not writing, she can be found with her nose firmly in a book, reliving the power of love in all walks of life. She can be contacted via her website, www.yvonnelindsay.com.

To Anna Campbell and Trish Morey,
the funniest "went to the cheese shop"
and French champagne buddies a girl could have!

One

"He's *dead?*"

Wade watched her carefully. Oh, she was a good actress all right. Anyone would think she was shocked, or even sorry, to hear her father had died. But if that was genuinely the case, maybe she'd have been at his side in his last hours instead of partying her way around the world these past eight years. He fought back the rawness of his own grief for the man who had been his mentor—his best friend. He should have been able to share that grief with the man's daughter. But he knew better than to share any part of his feelings with Piper Mitchell again.

"Yeah. Four days ago. This—" he gestured behind him to the throng of people circulating through the lower floors of the house "—is his wake."

"No, he can't be dead. You're lying." Piper took a shuddering breath. "You *have* to be lying!"

"I wouldn't waste my breath lying to you."

His words slowly sank in, digging beyond her disbelief.

He could see the exact moment the reality hit her. Her face paled beneath the healthy tan that had gilded her cheeks only moments ago. Her light-colored irises that glittered like the palest blue topaz all but disappeared as her pupils dilated and the shadows under her eyes hollowed and darkened. She took an unsteady step backward, and instinctively Wade shot out a hand to stop her before she toppled down the tiled stairs behind her.

She tilted her head to look at his hand, curled around her arm.

"I…I don't feel very well," she said, her voice trailing away into nothing as her knees buckled and her eyelids fluttered shut.

Silently cursing her for both her timing and her reaction, Wade scooped her up into his arms and carried her through the front door.

"Mr. Collins, is everything all right?" Dexter, the butler, for want of a better description, came hurrying from the ballroom where the bulk of the mourners had gathered over drinks and canapés.

"It's Miss Mitchell, she collapsed when she heard the news about her father," Wade replied, clamping his jaw on the more colorful adjectives he'd have preferred to use to explain her reaction.

"Should I call a doctor?" Dexter asked.

"No, I don't think that's necessary. Let's see how she feels when she wakes. Is her room still prepared?"

"It was one of Mr. Mitchell's express wishes that Miss Piper's room always be kept ready, sir."

"I'll take her up, then." Wade nodded at the pack Piper had dropped on the front porch. "Could you bring her things?"

"Certainly, sir."

Wade powered up the wide sweep of stairs with his late boss's daughter in his arms. Despite her height, she barely weighed enough to register on his breathing, and when he lay her down on the frilly comforter that adorned her bed, he noticed how thin and frail she was beneath the jeans and bulky sweatshirt she wore.

"Perhaps it would be best if I called Mrs. Dexter to attend to her," Dexter said smoothly as he deposited the grimy backpack on the polished wooden floor of the room.

"Yes," Wade said, watching for any signs of consciousness from the still inert form on the bed. There was no way he wanted to have his hands on her any longer than necessary. Not anymore. "That would be best."

Why now? he wondered. Why had she come back now? He stood to one side of the bed, watching the shallow rise and fall of her chest beneath the well-worn sweatshirt. He shook his head. He'd seen the bank statements and knew how she'd burned through her trust fund over the past eight years. What the hell had she spent all her money on? Certainly not clothing if what she wore now was anything to go by.

A noise at the door alerted him to the presence of the housekeeper-cum-cook he'd inherited along with Dexter when he'd bought the house from Rex Mitchell a couple years ago.

"Ah, lovey, what have you done to yourself?" Mrs. Dexter muttered under her breath as she pressed a hand to Piper's forehead. "And your beautiful hair, what on earth is this?"

"I believe they're called dreadlocks," Wade said dryly, his lip curling with derision.

Trust Piper to arrive on his doorstep looking like some refugee from another country. It was just the kind of plea for attention they'd all come to expect from her during her late teens.

Mind you, why should he be surprised? It amazed him to realize, deep down, he'd still hoped that she might have changed. But, no. In typical Piper fashion, she'd proven time and again that there was only one person who she cared about in this world, and that person was herself. And nothing and no one would ever get in the way of her pleasure. Not even her dying father.

Not even the baby she'd almost had.

Dexter reappeared in the doorway to Piper's room.

"Mr. Collins, your guests?"

"Yes, thank you, Dexter. I'll be down immediately."

Walking away from the woman on the bed, he returned to the gathering below. The gathering that was supposed to be a celebration of the life of the man who had given Wade every opportunity to shake off the dregs of his upbringing and excel. Rex Mitchell had been an ornery bastard at times, but he'd had a heart bigger than most and believed in rewarding hard work. And he'd loved his daughter, who had repaid him for that love by walking away from him without a backward glance. Sure, he'd tried to control Piper, but she'd been headstrong and needed a firm hand to guide her. For all the good that had done any of them.

Wade joined the throng in the ballroom of the stately home that was as much a part of Auckland's history as the families who had lived within its walls. He carried on, going through the motions, accepting messages of condolence, sharing stories that brought bittersweet smiles to everyone there. Finally, though, it all had to end and he was alone. Alone except for the Dexters, still clearing away glassware and dishes, and for the woman who'd remained upstairs.

Just when would she show her face again? he thought. Well, he wasn't in a hurry to force a confrontation. The outcome was bound to be less than pleasant.

He crossed the hall into the library, and made his way straight to the sideboard. The cognac gurgled satisfyingly from the neck of its bottle, the amber liquid splashing within the bowl of its receptor. Continuing the ritual he had enjoyed most evenings—before Rex's illness had left him weak and bed bound—Wade settled into the wingback chair beside the fire and lifted the glass in a silent toast to the empty chair on the other side.

"I see you couldn't wait to hit Dad's cognac."

Wade stiffened at the sound of Piper's voice from the entrance but he wouldn't give her the satisfaction of knowing how much she got under his skin with her choice of words. She, better than anyone, knew how he felt about alcohol and its disrespectful consumption.

"Care to join me?" he drawled in response, not even bothering to turn his face toward her.

"Sure, why not."

He heard her pour herself a measure then move across the hand-knotted carpet that covered the floor between them. With a tired sigh she settled into the chair that had been her father's. The fresh clean scents of soap and a light fragrance teased his nostrils. He cast her a glance. She'd showered and changed into a clean pair of jeans and a finely woven sweater. Beneath the fabric he could make out the lines of her bones. Even her face was more angular now. Harder, more experienced. A far cry from the spoiled young woman who'd taken his heart and crushed it beneath the soles of her feet when she'd walked out eight years ago.

"I can't believe he's really gone," she said softly.

He knew what she meant. Even he'd found it hard to face facts when Rex had handed the business reins over to him eighteen months ago. And before that, when Rex had negotiated the sale of his ancestral home to Wade to prevent it from sliding into a developer's hands after his death.

"Yeah, well, he is."

"I never thought he'd die."

"Neither did he, at first. The success rate for beating testicular cancer was in his favor."

"Cancer? I thought he died of a heart attack."

"What made you think that?"

"I don't know. I had no idea he was sick. I just assumed it was his heart. He always worked so hard."

Wade watched as her eyes washed with tears. He hadn't agreed with Rex's decision to withhold the details of his illness on the rare occasions Piper had made telephone contact. In recent months, the older man's stubbornness on the matter had been the only contentious bone between them. Rex hadn't believed Piper was strong enough to handle the stress of his illness, but with Piper as Rex's only living issue, Wade knew Rex deserved to have her there in his final days. And Wade hadn't really given a damn if she was strong enough for it or not.

Piper continued, "I'd have come home sooner had I known."

"Maybe that's part of why he didn't tell you," Wade retorted, her words just adding fuel to his frustration. She hadn't seen fit to share those last years of her father's life with him. Was it supposed to pacify Wade that she'd have been willing to come for Rex's death?

She bristled under his words, her eyes clearing instantly and the tears being swiftly replaced with a spark of anger.

"What do you mean by that?" Piper demanded.

"Exactly what I said. You know what your father was like. I'm not denying he wanted you home. He wanted that every day you were gone. But I think that deep down he still wanted you to come home because you wanted to, not because you had to."

"So you're saying I disappointed him—again." Her words were as defensive as the closed expression now on her face.

"Don't put words in my mouth, Piper." He expelled a frustrated huff of air, refusing to rise to her bait, and transferred his gaze to the fireplace. "Above everything, Rex always wanted to shelter you from the big bad world. In this last instance, that included his illness. He didn't want to put you through everything he was going through. Besides, it's all relative now, isn't it?"

"I think it's safe to say that we can take my father's continuing disappointment in me as a given," she said bitterly before taking a sip of her drink. "You, however, have remained the golden boy."

Piper fought back the urge to scream at Wade, to do something, anything to provoke him into a fight. After all, they'd had quite enough practice at it in their time together. It had always been that way between them. Passions running high, emotions deep. All of it crashing madly on the surface. A fight was something she could handle.

What she couldn't handle was the irrefutable truth that she'd never see her father again—never hear his booming voice through the home that had been in her family for generations, never feel the warmth of his arms clasping her to his barrel chest. The gaping hole that had taken up residence somewhere near her heart widened.

She would never have the chance to make it up to him for all the stress and emotional hardship she'd caused ever since, at the age of fourteen, she'd realized the power of her femininity. She knew he'd been sorry to see her leave for overseas shortly after she'd turned twenty, but she'd have been an idiot not to realize that his sorrow was tempered with relief at not having to deal with her, at times, appalling behavior in close quarters anymore.

Piper put down her glass on the small side table and pulled up her feet onto the seat, her knees tucked under her chin and her arms wrapped around her lower legs. How could he have kept his illness a secret from her like that? She'd had a right to know. He'd sounded tired the last time she'd called. When was that? Maybe three months ago? He should have told her.

A shaft of jealousy speared through her. He'd obviously shared everything with Wade. The two men had been close ever since Rex had taken on Wade as an intern at his export company. Wade had quickly become the son Rex had never had. The mythical son she'd never measured up to as Rex's only child.

She'd envied their closeness and done her level best to disrupt it—failing miserably in the process and irrevocably hurting the only two men she'd ever loved.

She hazarded a look at the man seated opposite her and felt that old familiar punch of desire. Even with that glowering expression on his face, he still had the power to make her nerves hum and her heart skip a beat. He'd certainly grown up since she'd been away. His face had settled into far more serious lines, and there was an edge to his jaw that the beginnings of a five o'clock shadow only enhanced. He filled out his designer suit with more breadth than he'd had before—it looked good on him. Clearly hard work and good living had served him well.

She flicked a glance to his left hand—no sign of a ring she noted—then castigated herself for even caring. He'd made his antipathy toward her quite clear. Besides, the new Piper Mitchell had determined to make amends for her past transgressions. Transgressions that included how she'd treated Wade, how she'd let her love for him make her selfish, demanding—wanting more from him than he was willing to give. She was so sorry now for the way she'd behaved, the choice she'd forced him to make between her and her father. Those amends needed to start now.

"I'm sorry," she said. "I know how much Dad meant to you, how close the two of you were. It must have been tough for you."

Wade looked at her, genuine surprise on his face. "Thank you," he answered.

There were fine lines of strain around his slate gray eyes that had never been there before. He looked thoroughly worn out.

"Did he suffer?"

Wade shook his head sharply. "Only inasmuch as he couldn't do what he wanted to do. The medical staff worked hard to keep him comfortable. He stayed here, at home, right to the end. We installed a hospital bed in the morning room and he had round-the-clock professional care."

"Thank you for being there for him."

"He'd have done it for me," Wade answered simply. "Besides, there was no place else I would rather have been."

And there it was again. The subtle slap. The reminder that she hadn't been there. Piper clamped down on her instinctive need to justify herself, her choices, her behavior. She was past that now. There was no way she could turn back time and rewrite history, but she could make a new beginning and that started here and now.

"I'm really grateful to know that he had you there. It must have meant a lot him. He always respected you."

"The feeling was mutual."

"So what happens now with the company?"

"What do you mean?" Wade looked surprised that she'd even asked.

"Well, you know, without Dad at the helm. Will everything be okay?"

"Yes, everything will be fine. Rex and I had a stable management plan in place before we knew he wasn't going to beat the cancer. I basically took over operations about a year and a half ago."

"Really?" Piper was surprised. "He let go that early?"

"It was a case of having to. The treatments, both here and overseas, left him pretty wiped out. But he maintained a keen interest in everything almost until the end. You know what Rex was like."

And where had she been a year and a half ago? Somalia? No, Kenya. She'd been helping at a women's clinic there. After that had been flood relief in Asia, then volunteering to help reconnect victims with their families after an earthquake in another devastated land. Everywhere but where she'd really needed to be. The one place where she should have made a difference.

Piper was suddenly hit with a massive weariness. She fought back a yawn and failed miserably.

"Still tired?" Wade asked.

"Yeah, when I got here I'd been traveling for about thirty-six hours. I don't think my body clock has caught up with the fact that I'm stationary yet."

"Why don't you go on up to your room? I'll get Mrs. Dexter to bring you a tray if you're hungry."

Despite all her good intentions, Piper bristled. This was her home, so who'd appointed him to the role of gracious host? If anything she should be offering him her hospitality under her father's roof. Reminding herself of her determination to be a better person, she swallowed the retort that hovered on the tip of her tongue. Instead she unfolded herself from the chair and stood up.

"Don't bother Dexie. I'll grab something from the kitchen on my way up."

She stretched slowly, easing out muscles that had been unused for far too long with all the travel she'd endured. She halted midstretch, suddenly aware of Wade's eyes locked onto her body. A long-suppressed, yet still familiar, tingle started deep inside and tendrils of heat began to unfurl from her core, radiating out to her extremities. She swallowed against the lump of tension that formed in her throat.

That old attraction was still there. Just as strong as ever. Did he feel the same way, too? Her eyes met his—for a moment seeing the same heat that had infused her body and now painted a faint flush against her suddenly warm cheeks. Then in an instant his eyes were the cool gray of indifference that had met her at the front door only a couple hours ago.

Stung by the clear rejection, Piper summoned every last ounce of dignity and offered him her hand.

"Thank you for everything you've done today."

Wade stood, his six feet two inches eclipsing her barefooted five feet eight. He took her hand in a brief clasp.

"I did it for Rex."

"I know that, and I appreciate it. Really."

He let go her hand as if the idea of holding it for a moment longer than necessary was abhorrent to him.

"Well," she said, gathering courage to her like a cloak, "I'll see you out and then I think I'll have an early night. No doubt I'll have plenty to do with the legal side of things tomorrow."

When Wade didn't make a move for the door, she speared him with a glance. "Is there something else you wanted to discuss?"

A slow smile, somewhat lacking in humor, spread across his handsome face.

"No," he replied. "I'll say good-night, then."

She watched as he left the room, but rather than heading toward the front vestibule he turned and made for the sweeping staircase that led to the upper floor.

"Where are you going?" she asked.

"To my room."

"To *your* room?"

His response was short and sweet. "I live here."

"Look, I appreciate that you probably stayed here for a while with Dad but that's not necessary now and, quite frankly, I'd really appreciate a bit of space and privacy to come to terms with everything."

"No problem. You're welcome to stay as long as you need to."

His answer left her baffled. "I beg your pardon?"

"I think you heard me, Piper. Despite your current appearance I'm sure you're not entirely stupid."

"How dare you!"

Better person be damned. That was quite enough. She'd already had to bear facing Wade for the first time since she had left him, not to mention hearing the news about her father's death. She wasn't about to stay and listen to him put her down, too.

"Look," she sputtered. "I think we both know there's enough history between us that your staying here is not a good idea."

"Probably." He shrugged. "But I think you may have misunderstood what I meant when I said I live here. Piper, I own the house. You're here as *my* guest."

Two

"You what?"

He owned the house? How could that be? The house had been built by her forebears in the mid-1800s. Passed on, generation by generation. Had Wade somehow finagled the property from her father while he was weakened by his illness? It seemed unlike him, but what else was she to think? His voice broke through her chaotic thoughts.

"Look, now probably isn't the best time to go into it. It's been a tough day all round. We can discuss this tomorrow."

"Like hell," she countered. "We can darn well discuss this right here, right now."

"If you insist," Wade said, closing the distance between them and gesturing toward the library. "Care to take a seat?"

With tension vibrating through every nerve in her body, Piper preceded him back into the room. She threw herself into the chair she'd only recently vacated, watching Wade as he lowered himself into his with far more elegance and grace than she'd exhibited. It only served to rankle even more.

"So, tell me. How is it you've come to be the owner of my father's house, and his before him, and his bef—"

Wade cut in. "Don't get melodramatic on me, Piper. It won't work."

Melodramatic? He thought *that* was melodramatic? That was nothing compared to how she felt right now. But before she could speak again, Wade continued.

"Your father and I came to a financial arrangement early on in his illness. The doctors here could offer little hope and he wanted to embark on some radical alternative therapy being offered overseas."

"What kind of arrangement?" she demanded. "And why on earth did he have to come to any kind of arrangement, anyway? Our family has always had money."

"*Had* being the operative word," Wade said, lifting his eyes to clash with hers.

"What? You're blaming me? I have my own trust fund. I was never a drain on my father's finances."

Wade's lips thinned and she saw a muscle clench in his jaw before he pushed a hand through his dark brown hair, sending the short cut into charming disarray. Despite her anger, her fingers itched to smooth his hair down—to feel if its texture was as smooth as she remembered it to be. Piper curled her fingers into her palms and squeezed tightly, ridding herself of the urge as quickly as it had surfaced. This wasn't the time to be thinking of any kind of touching.

"Not everything is about you, Piper. When you calm down, you'll see that what we did was supposed to be for the best, at the time."

"At the time? Explain it to me."

"Rex was single-minded about beating the disease and wouldn't take no for an answer, not even when his situation was very clearly laid out to him by his doctors. He was determined to fight, regardless of the cost—and the cost was very high. I've no idea what rock you've been hiding under for the past eight years but there has been a global recession out there. Our business was hit just as hard as everyone else's. Despite everything, there was a stage where we were bleeding money and Rex used a lot of his own funds to shore that up."

"You didn't use yours?" she asked pointedly.

"He wouldn't let me. Mitchell Exports was always *his* baby, you know that."

She probably knew it better than anyone. She'd always known that Rex's devotion to his business came well before his devotion to her.

"So he needed money for this treatment?" she probed.

"Yes, and he wouldn't take the money from me, even though I offered it freely. He was, however, happy to enter into a loan agreement with me, registering a mortgage in my name over the property."

"But this place is worth millions."

"He was very determined to live, Piper. He was prepared to pay whatever it took to beat the disease. At that stage, he never believed for a minute that he wouldn't live to pay me back."

"And he knew you already loved the property and would look after it."

Wade nodded slowly. "It was a more palatable solution for him than putting it on the open market to raise the funds, and seeing the land be gobbled up by developers, or risking borrowing the money through some financial institution and watching it go in a mortgagee sale if the treatment failed. When he knew he was going to die, he signed the property over to me in its entirety, provided he had a lifetime right to stay here. I had no problem with that."

Piper blinked back a new rush of tears. What Wade had said all sounded plausible. She knew how much her father had trusted Wade. Moreover, she knew—just as her father had known—how hard Wade's upbringing had been, how much he had wanted to prove he was better than his roots. If he'd been given the chance to demonstrate his friendship to Rex while simultaneously establishing himself in both the home and the business he'd always admired, then of course Wade had taken it. He was *right* to have taken it. But knowing that didn't take away the sick sense of loss Piper felt at the evidence that her father had given his entire legacy away to someone other than her.

If she'd been more determined to prove to her father that she was just as good as the son he'd always dreamed of having, if she'd stood by his side through the hard times instead of running away as soon as she didn't get her way, maybe she'd have been able to help him. But with her having remained overseas for as long as she had, often without any contact until she'd run out of money, again, and needed another advance from her funds, it was no wonder her father had sought a suitable custodian not only for his business but also for the house.

It didn't make it hurt any less, though. She'd never known another home and now she couldn't even call it hers anymore. Hopelessness hit her with a vengeance. Here she was, twenty-eight years old, no fixed abode, no job and no prospects. Sure, she still had her trust fund, but she didn't want to dip into that unless absolutely necessary. What on earth was she going to do?

"I meant what I said before, Piper," Wade said, his voice breaking into her tortured thoughts. "Rex asked me to look out for you. You're welcome to stay as long as you need to."

As long as she needed? How was she to know how long that was? She'd come back to New Zealand, back home, to restore the relationships she'd damaged so very badly with her selfish decisions and past behaviors. The past four years, volunteering with aid relief in less privileged countries, had been a major eye-opener. One that had systematically changed her focus and made her realize just how empty her life had been and how much she continued to owe the people who'd been a part of it. People who she'd only later realized had tried to give her the love and stability she'd always craved. People she'd cast off in her anger and hurt for not loving her the way she'd wanted, oblivious to the fact that she was hurting them with her actions, too. People like her father, and Wade.

"Thank you," she said softly.

What else was there to say? She was at his mercy. He had every right to turn her out of the house.

"If there's nothing else, I'll say good-night," Wade answered.

He rose from his seat and started to leave the room, hesitating a moment at the door as if he had something more to say. But then, with an almost imperceptible shake of his head, he continued into the hallway.

Around her, Piper heard the wooden timbers of the hundred-and-sixty-year-old home settle in the cooling night air. A sound she'd never even stopped to listen to before, yet a sound that was a solid reminder of all who'd been before her and left their mark on her world. Their expectations lay heavy in the atmosphere that filled the room. What mark had she left?

The emptiness around her invaded the hollows of her body and echoed through to her soul.

Nothing. She'd left nothing.

She drew a shaky breath deep into her lungs. Then another. She'd made a conscious choice to change her life. No one ever said it was going to be easy or that she'd have all the things at her disposal that she'd always taken for granted. Maybe this was one of the lessons she needed to learn along the way. Take nothing, and no one, for granted.

Piper moved down the hallway, her bare feet making no sound on the faded carpet runner that lined the polished wooden floor. She hesitated outside the morning room, unsure of what she'd find there. What remnants of her father's illness and care from during his last days would linger? And what of the hospital bed and equipment Wade had said they'd set up in here?

She wasn't surprised he'd chosen this room. It had purportedly been her mother's favorite. Not that she remembered her mother beyond a vague sense of being enveloped in soft arms and being showered with butterfly kisses. Sometimes, as a child, she'd come in here and curl up on a chair with her eyes shut tight—trying to gain a sense of the woman who'd borne her. But try as she might, she had never felt any more than that elusive memory.

Her hand hovered over the brass doorknob until with a sudden resolution, she closed her fingers around the cold metal and gave it a twist. The door swung open before her revealing a room unchanged from the last time she'd seen it.

The chaise longue still resided in front of the French doors that opened onto the wraparound veranda. The side tables and comfortable furniture she remembered as far back as her childhood were all still there.

She sniffed the air carefully. No, not a hint of hospital or illness, or death, remained. It was as if her father had never been in here at all.

A solid lump of grief built in her throat as she stepped back and closed the door again. She desperately wanted some connection with him. Some proof that despite everything he'd still loved her.

Noises from the kitchen at the back of the house reminded her that Dexter and his wife were hard at work cleaning up after her father's wake. She should go to them. Offer to help. But the need to be alone with her thoughts was stronger. She turned and made her way back along the hallway and then up the stairs that led to the bedrooms on the next floor.

Rex's room had been at the opposite side of the house from hers. When her mother had died when Piper was three, he'd hired a nanny who'd slept in the room next to hers. But he'd kept his distance for many years, physically, emotionally and socially. It was only when she'd begun to bring certificates of achievement home from school that he'd really begun to acknowledge her existence, spurring her to do better, reach higher—whatever it took to garner his approval.

But that approval was always short-lived as his work took the bulk of his attention. She'd always wanted for him to see her as more than a child to be spoiled, her every whim indulged. She'd wanted him to acknowledge that she had a brain, that she could achieve, even that she might be worthy one day of working with him in the family business as he would have expected a son to do. Instead, no matter how high she flew academically, it was as if her achievements never really mattered to him. After that, behaving like the spoiled little princess he expected had become second nature—in fact, she'd almost turned it into an art form. For all the good it did her.

Piper bypassed her own room and headed toward the rooms that had been his. The door to his suite was open. She stepped into her father's domain and was instantly enveloped by his personality. The room was neat and tidy, typical of the ordered way he'd liked things, but here and there were the memories she'd always associated with him. The books he had loved to read, the sweets he had kept in a porcelain jar beside the bed for "just in case."

Pulling open his wardrobe, Piper was assailed with the faint reminder of the cologne he'd always worn. She reached for the dressing gown that hung on the hook on the back of the door and dragged it to her, burying her face in the velvet softness of the fabric and inhaling deeply.

"Is everything okay?"

She spun around to see Wade framed in the doorway, the light from the hall behind him, leaving his face in shadow. He looked as if he was in the process of getting undressed. Gone were his jacket and tie. His shirt buttons were now open halfway down his chest, his shirt untucked from the sharply creased trousers that encased his long legs, the cuffs undone and loose around his strong wrists.

Longing for what-might-have-been hit her in a surge of confused emotion. She shook her head slightly, trying to dislodge the sensations that clouded her mind. Comfort. She craved comfort, that most basic of needs. But she could no more ask that of Wade than she could ask for the moon, not after what had happened between them. Not when she still had so much making up to do. So much to prove—to him and to herself.

"I'm fine. Just..." What? It was impossible to put into words. Instead she settled for the benign. "I miss him. Why didn't he give me the chance to come back earlier and say goodbye?"

In the doorway, Wade shifted on his feet. She sensed there was more he wanted to say but that he was holding back.

"Like I said before, he didn't want you to have to go through it all. To have to watch him deteriorate. Maybe it was a bit of pride, too, wanting you to remember him as he was when you left rather than when he was so ill."

"He never really expected me to come back, did he?"

Wade shook his head slightly. "No, I don't think he ever did. Didn't stop him wanting you here, though."

The light from the hall shone into the room, bathing Piper in a stream of golden light. She looked so vulnerable there, holding her father's robe to her as if it was some form of security blanket. As if it was the last remaining thing she had left in the world. Well, truth be told, it pretty much was. Still, she didn't need to know that now. Time enough for that. Even he could see she was struggling with the reality of Rex's death. Hell, he'd been here, through it all, and he still struggled.

He clamped down on the sympathy that came as naturally to him as breathing. The past few days he'd doled out his fair share to Rex's friends and business associates. Offering solace to Piper should have been just one more drop in the bucket. But, he reminded himself, she'd made choices that made it difficult to dredge up any consolation for her. One choice in particular he could never forgive was that she'd chosen to end the life they'd created together before he'd ever known it had existed. He'd sworn she'd pay dearly for that choice. She owed him now in ways she couldn't begin to imagine.

Even with that mental reminder, his hands itched to reach out to her, to touch her, comfort her. He'd been so in love with her once, and as angry as he still was with Piper, those old instincts dominated. Wade curled his hands into fists and thrust them inside his trouser pockets lest he give into them. He had no doubt she'd take what he offered—before throwing it right back in his face all over again.

She'd made it monumentally clear during their last bitter and very final argument, before she went overseas, that she needed nothing from him. Even her demeanor downstairs when she'd joined him in the library had been targeted to make him feel inferior, an outsider.

He leaned against the doorjamb, marshaling his thoughts and reminding himself that her vulnerability was little more than a facade. Piper Mitchell was more than capable of handling herself in any situation. She'd suckered him in once before and he'd vowed he would not be a fool twice over her.

He shook his head slightly to clear his mind of the errant thought. He'd been under a lot of pressure. That was all. He just needed time to get his bearings again, to sort through what still needed to be done about Rex's estate and to put a lid on his grief until it no longer had the capacity to render him weak, or open to confusing thoughts about Piper.

Wade cleared the thickness in his throat and took one hand from his pocket and gestured toward the room.

"I've been charged with clearing out your father's things. Do you want to help with that?"

She nodded, a mere incline of her head. The action typical Piper, too wrapped up in her own thoughts to give anyone her full attention. But in the gloom he heard a noise that sounded suspiciously like a choked sob.

"Look, it's been a tough day," he continued. "Why don't you head off to bed? There's no hurry with your dad's things."

"Okay, but don't get rid of anything before I can see it."

Ah, so despite that faint wobble in her voice she was back to giving orders. That hadn't taken long. "Sure," he said, denuding his voice of its last threads of empathy. "By the way, I have an appointment with Rex's lawyers in the morning for the official reading of the will—you should come along. I'm already conversant with its contents but you should probably take the opportunity to find out exactly how you're placed."

She nodded. "Sounds like a good idea."

Wade stepped aside as she approached, but Piper's foot caught on the edge of the carpet square, making her stagger. Instinctively, as he had already done once today, he put out a hand to steady her, shifting his body to block her fall. Again, her weight bore against him, seeking support. She looked up at him, her eyes dull with sorrow.

"Thank you. I'm going to have to stop making a habit of this, aren't I?"

"Might be an idea," he conceded, even as his body warmed instantly to the feel of her.

He put his hands to her shoulders. It would be so easy to attempt to recapture that old spark simply by lowering his mouth to hers. Her lips were already parted on a hitched breath, their softness moist and enticing. Her pupils rapidly consuming the pale color of her irises.

The firm roundness of her breasts pressed against his chest and his body surged to aching life. Wade silently cursed himself for being all kinds of a fool. His hunger had been tamped down and controlled for far, far too long. Beneath his hands her body stiffened, freezing in response to his very obvious physical reaction to her nearness.

His hands tightened, his breath catching in his chest as he fought his demons. She had always been temptation incarnate. But he was stronger now. Stronger and more determined to succeed—in all things.

Even though his entire body pulsed with wanting her—wanting to push aside the shabby clothing she wore and to rediscover the creamy smoothness of her skin, the warm recesses of her body that held incalculable delight—he pushed her gently from him. It was sobering to realize that passion had threatened, albeit briefly, to blot out his every reasonable thought.

Piper pulled farther back, her arms still wrapped around that damn robe. It occurred to him that throughout their entire embrace, she hadn't voluntarily touched him with any part of her body. He shoved one hand through his hair.

"So, until tomorrow then?" she said, the lightness in her voice sounding forced in the heavily charged air between them.

"Tomorrow?"

"The lawyer? What time should I be ready?"

"The appointment isn't until midmorning. No need to rush."

"Okay, I'll probably see you at breakfast, then."

She slipped past him and down the hall to her room. He watched her every step—the graceful posture, the gentle sway of her hips.

They said that revenge was a dish best served cold, but he preferred his steaming hot. Hot and sexy and totally satisfying on all counts. He *would* be vindicated. And, when the time was right, he would savor every moment.

In her room, Piper sat heavily onto her bed and raised her fingers to her lips. She'd been so sure he was going to kiss her.

She'd have almost staked her life on it. The flare of desire in his eyes had been so endearingly familiar that it had shaken her to her core—had awakened her senses, her own needs— in a way she hadn't experienced for a very long time.

She knew he'd wanted her—she'd felt the undeniable evidence against her. So what had made him stop? One minute he'd been conciliatory, the next cool and commanding and then he'd been on fire for her. A fire she'd all-too-readily reciprocated. Even now, her skin felt too tight. Her nerve endings too close to the surface. She pushed up from the bed and paced her room, suddenly filled with an excess of energy that begged for some form of release.

Who was she kidding? She knew exactly what form of release she craved. And with whom. But it wasn't going to happen. Wade had always had the power to turn her inside out, right from the first time she'd laid eyes on him. The instant physical attraction had rapidly morphed into one that went infinitely deeper. She had no doubt they would be as compatible now as they'd been before, but she couldn't allow herself to go down that path. It would undoubtedly lead to broken promises and broken hearts all over again and she had resolved to put things right when she came home. Put things right and prove herself to be the kind of person she most wanted to be. Not the selfish creature of the past who sought satisfaction for her every desire, but someone who could genuinely contribute to the world in which she lived and moved.

It hurt deep, deep down that she'd never be able to prove to her father that she was capable of being more than what he'd pigeonholed her to be. What she'd shamefully allowed herself to become in the face of his opposition to her gaining a career that could amount to something. He'd loved her, but he'd never had any understanding or appreciation for the person she had the potential to be. It was too late to show him otherwise. But she could prove it to herself.

She shook her head. How was she ever going to prove herself if she couldn't control even her most basic urges around Wade?

Piper stopped pacing in front of the built-in bookcase that lined one wall of her room. It was still adorned with the things she'd grown up with. Her previous life had been sealed in a time capsule, waiting for her return. She looked around, seeing everything with new eyes.

Her gaze stopped on one of the collections of porcelain dolls her father had insisted on buying for her, but had never let her play with. What a perfect analogy for her life, she thought bitterly. Look but don't touch. Learn, but whatever you do, don't use that knowledge. Be beautiful, but don't actually *be* anything.

She drew in a deep breath and squared her shoulders. Well, all that was going to change. As much as she'd loved her father, and had strived for his attention, she could see that they were equally to blame for her past behavior. But she had changed and she planned to continue to change and grow a whole lot more. Including going back to university and finishing her degree.

It had taken quite a bit to make her eventually grow up. Being overseas alone, facing her darkest days and subsequently her brightest moments as she'd reawakened to who she needed to be.

Still, she had to attend to her father's estate first, and that meant getting up on time to see the lawyer tomorrow morning, which in turn meant getting a decent night's sleep.

She went through the motions of getting ready for bed, finding solace in routine and joy in the things she used to take so much for granted. Simple things, like a tube of toothpaste, running water from a tap, a flush toilet. She laughed at her reflection in the mirror. Who'd have thought that Piper Mitchell would ever have been reduced to this? Finding joy in modern plumbing. Frankly, she didn't care, not anymore.

The toll of the news she'd borne today, and the travel she'd undertaken to get here, swamped her and the lure of fresh clean sheets and a proper bed became stronger than she could resist.

The next morning, Piper woke as the sun began to filter through her window. To her surprise she had tears on her cheeks and her pillow was damp beneath her face. She'd been dreaming about her father and the sense of forever being left reaching out for him, yet not being accepted by him, still filled her. She swiped a hand across her face. Tears wouldn't solve anything, she knew that with an entrenched awareness she'd learned the hard way. No matter the loss, you had to learn to get through it.

She rolled to the other side of her bed and stretched, luxuriating in the sensation of fine cotton sheeting against her bare skin. Her father's robe was spread over the top of her bed and she grabbed it to her, pulling it on as she sat up and slipped from between the sheets to make her way into the adjoining bathroom.

Eschewing a shower for the decadence of a deep bath, she bent over and turned on the faucets. Watching the water fill in the ancient claw-footed tub gave her an illicit sense of pleasure. She would never take something like this for granted again. Despite everything that had happened since her return, it was so incredibly good to be home.

Hard on the heels of that thought came the reminder that the house was no longer her home. She was a guest here. Wade's guest. The news had come as a shock last night and her reaction had been instinctive and out of sorts with her new resolve. She hoped that would be the last unpleasant surprise she'd have to bear.

She was in a painfully tenuous situation. She had no qualifications to speak of, unless bartering with local rebels or militia for medical supplies and trading with cash from her trust fund was anything worth mentioning. Nor did she now have a roof over her head to call her own.

Piper slipped the robe off her shoulders and, letting it drop to the floor behind her, stepped into the almost full bath. She sank into the water, letting its warmth seep into her skin all the way through to her bones. After the heat of some of the countries she'd lived in, she didn't think she'd still crave warmth the way she did now. But with her father dead and her prospects perched on a very precarious ledge, the world around her felt very cold indeed.

Piper let her hair fall over the back of the bath and rested her head against the edge, closing her eyes and trying to concentrate only on the warmth and softness of the water enclosing her body. She'd found the exercise of isolating herself to be an invaluable tool in coping with some of the hardships she'd witnessed in the past few years, but for some reason she couldn't find quite the degree of separation she needed now.

Where she was going to live, how she was to support herself, all took precedence over her relaxation ritual. It wasn't as if she didn't still have the trust fund her mother had left her, she rationalized. Her father had been angry with her when she'd gone overseas, especially when she'd tried to get between him and Wade, but he hadn't cut her off completely. Whenever she'd applied for an advance from the funds she'd come into when she'd turned eighteen, the money had duly appeared wherever she'd needed it. By her reckoning she should still have sufficient capital left to get herself on her feet, certainly enough to finish the degree she'd partially completed before running away.

She grimaced. *Running away* sounded so infantile. And yet, her reactions had been those of a spoiled brat. She wasn't proud of the person she'd been then. Not at all. But that was changing. Slowly, surely and in the right direction. And with the balance of her funds behind her, the rest would be a piece of cake.

She felt a pang of grief tug deep inside her. How she wished her father was still alive. Maybe he could finally have been proud of her, *really* proud. She missed him with a sorrow that went soul-deep. When she'd set out on the journey home, she'd been looking forward to seeing him again. She'd hoped with all her heart that today could be the first stage of a new relationship with her dad. One where he would finally see who she was and what she was capable of.

Well, she still hovered at the edge of that first stage. One she'd have to embark on for herself, not for anyone else. It was what she should have realized all along.

Piper pulled the plug on the bath and stepped out as the water swirled down the drain with a satisfying gurgle. She shook her head at the decadence of it. It would make better sense to find some way to utilize the waste water from this sort of thing on the property. Maybe she could make some suggestions to Wade and see what he thought. He'd probably have a hard time believing she could even care about something like waste water.

Piper dried herself off and padded naked into her bedroom. She extracted some clean underwear from her drawer, a small puzzled frown fracturing her brow when she couldn't find the stuff she'd brought in her backpack. The pack itself had been emptied at some stage yesterday, its clothing contents now nowhere to be found. Maybe Mrs. Dexter had taken it all to be washed, she thought. She wondered what the housekeeper would think of the wardrobe that consisted mainly of jeans, camo-patterned trousers and an array of T-shirts that would probably better serve as polishing cloths than anything else.

She looked at the underwear she'd taken from the drawer. An exquisite shell pink, the matching bra and panties were a brand she'd never bought before, even though they were all in the size she'd worn before she went away. She slipped into the panties, thankful that at least they fit without threatening to fall off her hips, then adjusted the straps on the bra and started to put it on.

She turned and looked at herself in the mirror. She'd lost weight in recent years. Hard work and a limited diet had a way of doing that. The bra, while beautiful, was far too big for her, even on the tightest fitting. She could pad it up, she supposed, but then what if something slid free while she was wearing it? No, far better to go without, she decided and turned to her old wardrobe for something to wear.

A swimming sense of déjà vu enveloped her as she opened the doors. There, arranged by color and functionality, hung every article of clothing she'd failed to pack and take away with her. According to the dry cleaning tags on the garments, everything had been freshened recently. But why, when no one knew when she was coming home?

Piper selected the least flippant items and pulled on a pair of charcoal gray trousers with a neat matching jacket that used to nip in perfectly at her waist. Eight years ago, it had been form-fitting enough to wear without a top beneath it, but it certainly wasn't now. She flicked through the hangers until she found a crisp white blouse to team with it.

An old belt threaded through the loops in her trousers cinched them in a little tighter at her waist, and when Piper pulled on the jacket and studied her appearance, she thought she'd scrubbed up quite well—aside from the hair. She grabbed a black and white long silk scarf from her dresser and tied her dreads into an approximation of a ponytail before nodding at her reflection. Well enough to see the lawyer, anyway.

Her feet had always been long and narrow and she pulled on a pair of stocking socks before pushing her feet into a slim fitting pair of black patent pumps. No longer used to the heels, she teetered a little before regaining her composure.

How had she ever walked in these things on a daily basis? she wondered as she made her way down the stairs.

Wade wasn't in the breakfast room, nor the kitchen, when she got downstairs.

"Looking for Mr. Collins?" Mrs. Dexter said with a smile as she bustled about pouring a fresh cup of tea and placing it at Piper's old place at the huge worn kitchen table.

"Yes, we have an appointment together this morning."

"He had to get away early to the office. Some problem or other. He said if he couldn't get back on time, he'd send a car for you so you could still meet with Mr. Chadwick in his rooms."

"Oh, thanks."

Piper fought back the unreasonable feeling of disappointment that he wasn't here. He had a business to run so she could hardly expect him to wait upon her hand and foot. Strangely, though, she had been looking forward to his approval that she'd made an effort to "scrub up," for want of a better term. Which reminded her. Her clothes.

"Dexie, can you tell me what you did with my clothing from my backpack?"

"Oh, that lot." Mrs. Dexter wrinkled up her nose in her rosy cheeked face. "I gave it all to Dexter to incinerate. Your father would never have stood for you dressing like that."

Piper bit back the retort that her father hadn't had the right to dictate her appearance for many years now. Swallowing the words she'd wanted to say didn't come easy. Those items of clothing were virtually all she'd had to her name in the way of physical possessions. She'd come back here to take control of her life and yet, even in something as simple as her clothing, she'd been railroaded.

"Besides," the older woman continued, "you have a wardrobe full of beautiful things to wear. I must say, lovey, it's wonderful to see you looking more your old self. Apart from the hair, that is."

A wry smile formed at Piper's lips. "You don't like it?" she teased.

"Humph, as if Mr. Mitchell would ever have tolerated such a thing."

Piper's smile died on her face. No, her father wouldn't have tolerated it. He wouldn't have understood the sheer practicality of wearing her hair this way in the circumstances in which she'd lived. Now she was home she supposed she'd better do something about it, but first there was the appointment today to get through.

"Get through" being the operative words, she realized later that day as her father's lawyer sat opposite her at his highly polished desk, a sobering expression on his face.

"What do you mean I have no money?" she demanded. "When I left, my trust fund was healthy. It had been operating since my mother's death, earning interest all the way. Surely I didn't spend it all?"

"No, Miss Mitchell, you didn't. But you didn't exactly use the funds wisely, or reinvest, either, did you?"

It felt as if she'd been victimized from the instant she'd arrived home. First Wade, then Dexie's disapproval, and now this.

"They were mine to use," she said, a defensive note in her voice.

"Of course, of course." The old man made a shushing sound in a vain attempt to placate her.

But Piper would not be placated.

"So where is it?"

"It?"

"The money," she clarified, holding onto her temper by a thread.

"You know that with your father as a Trustee, the funds were managed very carefully. Over the years he frequently diversified the investments, but as you must be aware, financial markets worldwide have been hit very hard. Even investments that appeared to be sound suffered, and you subsequently lost some rather large sums."

Piper shook her head. She couldn't believe what she was hearing. Her father had always been the most prudent and cautious of investors.

"So, I have nothing?"

"I'm so very sorry."

"But what about my father's estate?"

"Miss Mitchell, what your father didn't use to carry Mitchell Exports through some tough times, he used to fund alternative treatments for his illness. There really is very little left. The investment losses your fund endured hit him, also."

Everything Wade had told her last night had been true. She wished she could blame him, hold him responsible for her father's weak financial position at the time of his death, but it was clear Wade had conducted himself the same way he always had. With honor and loyalty to the man he revered above all others.

Mr. Chadwick continued, completely unaware of the turmoil in her mind. "I must say that Mr. Collins has been most benevolent. When he realized the situation your father was facing he personally acted to assist him. Rex was fortunate that Mr. Collins was compassionate enough to give him a lifetime right to reside in the house."

The sick taste of bile rose in Piper's throat.

Piper swallowed. "And my mother's art collection? That should have been left to me in my father's will. What has happened to that?"

At least if she had that, all was not lost. As much as she hated the idea of selling a single piece, she'd be able to liquidate some funds.

"All with Mr. Collins now. I understand the collection is on loan to the Sydney Art Gallery at the moment."

"But it wasn't my father's to give. It was supposed to be mine."

She fought to keep the panic from her voice. Without the collection, she really had nothing.

"Under the terms of your mother's will, it was your father's to dispose of at his discretion. While she stipulated her preference that it be given to you when you reached your majority, it was still left to your father to decide in the end. Some years ago, he mentioned to me that he had some concerns that you might feel compelled to break the collection up and he wanted to avoid that at all costs. Moreover, he wanted to be certain you were settled before entrusting it to you. In all fairness to your father, he honestly expected your trust fund to support you for your lifetime. Hardly anyone foresaw the long-term ramifications of the global financial crisis until it was too late."

Piper slumped in the chair. Her life couldn't get any worse, could it?

"There is one other thing," the lawyer said carefully, making all the hairs on the back of her neck stand on end.

Piper sat up. She didn't like the way he'd prefaced what was coming next. There was something in his posture and tone that warned her that what she'd learned already was small-fry compared to what was coming next.

"Tell me," she demanded. She may as well get it straight on the chin now.

"Your trust fund. With your withdrawals and the depreciation of the investments' value over time, it became overdrawn. Mr. Collins had taken charge of your father's affairs by that point, and personally advanced money to the fund to cover the shortfall when he was made aware of the situation."

"Just how much money did he advance?"

The lawyer named a sum that caused black spots to swim before her eyes.

"So you're saying he advanced several hundred thousand dollars to my trust fund?"

Wade had been the one responsible for the money she'd used to finance schools and health clinics, food and clothing and farm supplies in the counties she'd visited in the past four years? She was struck with an urgent need to understand the conditions of the loan and expressed as much to Mr. Chadwick.

"The loans were rather open-ended. As your trustee, your father entered into deeds acknowledging the debt between the fund and Mr. Collins. Obviously Mr. Collins has the right to recall those loans, with interest, at any time."

"So no repayments have been made to date?"

"None, Mr. Collins hadn't requested such repayment."

"Not at all?"

She was confused. How could anyone afford to make such huge sums of money available like that and not expect something back in return?

"No, not at all." Chadwick hesitated a moment, his mouth twisting into a moue of regret. "Until now."

"Now?" she gasped. "He wants me to repay the debt now?"

"Yes, Miss Mitchell, I'm afraid so. And he has specified it must be repaid in full."

Three

In full? Piper vibrated with ill-concealed anger, earning a look of concern from the elderly man across the table from her. No wonder Wade had arranged to not be at the appointment with her, the rat.

"Thank you," she finally managed to say through gritted teeth. "Could you tell me exactly *when* Wade Collins made that specification?"

"We received his instruction this morning."

This morning? It was unbelievable. While she'd been sleeping in, or even while she'd been lazing about in her bath, he'd been demanding she clear a debt he knew full well she had no ability to repay.

Forcing a smile on her face, she stood and offered her hand to the man who'd been her father's longtime legal counsel.

"Is there anything I can do for you, Miss Mitchell?"

"Short of conducting a miracle, I doubt it."

She kept her composure until she got outside the office and saw the car Wade had ordered for her waiting in the loading zone outside. Every instinct within her urged her to turn in the opposite direction and to keep walking. To put as much distance as possible between herself and the awful truth about her financial position. But where would she go?

The driver of the car got out and came around to the passenger side, opening the door for Piper and waiting until she'd settled herself in the soft leather. The drive back to the house passed in a blur. She couldn't have said whether they'd taken one route or another but when they drove into the long driveway that led to the imposing stairs and entrance to the house, Piper found her eyes locked on the building she'd grown up in.

The immaculate white painted woodwork, the wraparound verandas on the ground and next story, the green-capped pinnacles that marked the four corners of what had begun as a two-story farmhouse. She'd taken every part of it for granted. Its history, its shelter, its place in her life.

She had thought she'd changed, but she hadn't changed at all. Even without a home to call her own, she'd still assumed she had the money to make a new one. But now she didn't have even that. And all because she'd been so stupidly presumptuous as to believe her security would never end.

So what now? She didn't even appear to own the clothes on her back, and Dexter had destroyed what little she had owned.

Piper slowly moved up the stairs and let herself in through the front door. She started as a tall shadow materialized from the formal parlor on her left.

"Wade," she said. "I wasn't expecting you here."

"I managed to clear things up at the office earlier than I'd anticipated."

Her eyes raked his face for any sign of the man who'd deliberately advanced money to her only to recall it when he knew she was at her lowest ebb. Just how long had he been prepared to go on making money available to her? she wondered. If she hadn't come back when she did, how much would she have ended up owing him?

It didn't make sense. She had no way of paying him back. Why would he want to have such a hold over her when it was outside the realm of possibility that she'd ever earn enough money to settle the debt?

"Is that right?" she replied, fighting to keep her voice level when all she wanted to do was bombard him with angry questions.

"I take it the news at the lawyer's wasn't good?"

"You take it correctly."

"We should talk."

"No kidding," she said with an insolence she was incapable of hiding.

Wade gestured for her to precede him into the parlor and waited until she was seated before he lowered his body into one of the fabric-covered armchairs. The blowsy cabbage rose pattern on the chair was at complete odds with his controlled appearance. Not a hair was out of place on his head. His striped tie, a perfect match to the steel gray of his suit, was immaculately knotted at the equally immaculate fold of the collar of the white shirt he wore. He was altogether formidable, and he knew it.

Piper decided to take the bull by the horns.

"It would appear I owe you some money," she said, lifting her gaze to meet his squarely. There was no way she would show him that she was quaking inside.

To her surprise, Wade laughed. His even white teeth flashed in his face, his eyes crinkled in genuine mirth and the sound, a deep belly laugh that in any other circumstance would have been infectious, rang out to fill the room.

"I have to hand it to you, Piper. You're the mistress of understatement today."

She refused to be drawn to respond. He could think what he liked. He knew, as well as she did, that he held all the cards very firmly in those beautiful hands of his. While he composed himself she waited patiently for the bullet to come.

"Mr. Chadwick made you aware of the sum of money you owe me," he finally said, his voice no longer holding any hint of the humor that had just consumed him.

"He did."

"And he made you aware that the debt has been recalled."

"With interest, no less," she said, aiming for flippancy.

Maybe if she could make him angry she'd feel anything but the numbness that had pervaded her entire body since she'd heard the news.

"No less," he agreed.

He sat back in his chair and rested his hands on the arms of it, his rangy body relaxed even though his eyes were sharply focused on her face.

"I need time," she stated flatly.

"Is that a fact?"

"Of course it's a fact," she snapped, rising to his bait in spite of her best intentions. "I need time to find a job, get established. It's completely unreasonable of you to insist on repayment in full when I have no means to meet that commitment."

"Yes, indeed. Thing is—" he paused and flicked an imaginary piece of lint from his trouser leg "—I don't feel particularly reasonable right now."

A chill ran down Piper's spine. "You don't?"

"No, I don't. You never finished university, despite every opportunity to do so. You never sought gainful employment while in New Zealand. And if your current lack of funds is any indication, I'd say you've never actually worked a day in your life. Why should I believe that you could find a job now? The employment market is tough, Piper. Tougher now than it ever was. Even the local supermarkets have had more than two and a half thousand applicants for each of the new stores that have opened recently. What makes you think you're better than all those skilled, and unskilled, workers desperate to find a job?"

"I never said I was better than anyone else."

"No, you didn't. At least not recently, anyway."

Piper felt hot color flood her cheeks. She remembered exactly what he referred to. She'd been an utter bitch to him when he'd refused to drop his internship with her father and travel with her overseas. She'd wanted him to prove that he loved her—that she mattered to him more than her father and his own future. When he'd refused, she'd said things that didn't deserve remembering, let alone repeating. That he hadn't forgotten them was quite clear.

"I'm sorry for all that, Wade. I really am. I was young, headstrong and entirely stupid. I couldn't see past what I wanted back then."

"And you've changed so much now?"

Wade watched her carefully. He didn't believe she'd changed a bit. Not where it mattered. She could have swallowed her pride years ago. Come home before choosing to terminate the pregnancy that was the lingering proof of the love he'd thought they'd shared. But, no. She'd destroyed his son or daughter as callously as she'd cast away everything in their relationship. And she hadn't even bothered to contact him—then, or in the eight years that had followed.

"I have changed," she insisted, the color in her cheeks rising. The sound of her voice becoming even more impassioned. "I used that money for good purpose."

"All of it?"

"No, not all of it. I was an idiot when I left here. I had some serious growing up to do, but I did grow up. I have changed."

"Admitting your faults all sounds very impressive, Piper, but again, none of it solves your current problem, does it?"

"I just need time."

"Time isn't an option." He put up a hand before she could

protest. "I do, however, have an alternative for you. A suggestion that takes into account your lack of credible work experience and probably accommodates the one thing I *do* know you're good at."

She leaned forward on her seat, clearly eager to hear what he had to say. He doubted she'd be as eager once she knew what he had planned for her.

"What sort of alternative?"

"I worked hard for your father over the years. And with your father gone, my workload has doubled at Mitchell Exports.

"As a result, I have neither the time, nor the inclination, to devote to a relationship with the type of woman I may want as a wife. Settling down just isn't possible for me right now. But I do have one thing, above all else, that I wish for.

"I've accumulated quite a legacy of my own, now, and it'll be all for nothing unless there is someone special in my life to leave it to. You know about how my mother died when I was ten and how my father refused to support me. You know how determined that made me to have children who will receive all my love and protection. I want to be the kind of father Rex was to you. When you were a toddler and your mother died he never let you go. It would have been far easier for him to have done so. Yet, no matter what, he always provided for you—sometimes too much."

"Our circumstances are completely different, Wade. Sure, Dad supported me, but not in all the ways that really mattered to *me*. I had to fight for his attention."

"He wasn't always the easiest of men to impress, but he never stopped loving you, Piper. Never. Have you stopped to wonder why your room was still exactly the same as you left it? Why you have new clothing in your drawers and why the things in your wardrobe have been regularly dry cleaned for when you eventually returned home? Keeping everything in readiness for you was probably the only way he knew to show you how much you meant to him. But you never came home."

Wade sighed and rubbed his eyes with one hand. "We're diverting from my point. What I wanted to say is that family is *everything* to me. I want to have a child to make all this hard work worthwhile. Someone I can leave my legacy to."

To his surprise Piper shot to her feet, coming to stand a bare meter from him.

"And I suppose this legacy includes all those things that were supposed to be mine. Things like my mother's art collection?"

"Things I have legitimate bills of sale for, yes."

"Where do I come into all of this?"

He remained silent, waiting for the penny to drop. It didn't take long.

"You want me to have your baby?" she cried, staggering back as if she'd sustained a physical blow.

"You're rejecting my suggestion?"

"Damn right I'm rejecting it."

"It's not what I'd call an ideal situation but I'm prepared to waive the considerable debt you owe me, if you give me a child."

He stood and closed the distance between them. A pulse fluttered frantically in her throat and her breath came in short bursts. Beneath her jacket he could see the unfettered rise and fall of her breasts against the fine linen of her blouse. A rush of heat swelled from deep within him.

He continued, "We're not completely repulsive to one another. It's not likely to be any hardship to do what needs to be done to meet your end of the deal."

"You're talking about a baby! A living, breathing human being. Not just some pawn in a game of chess."

"I know exactly what I'm talking about, Piper. The thing is, are you up for the challenge?"

Piper stared at him in horror. Did he have any idea what he

was asking of her? It was wrong on so many levels she could barely gather her wits. She wasn't ready to have a baby. Not now—maybe not ever. The word "no" echoed through her mind. In fact, it was on the tip of her tongue, ready to burst forth, when he spoke.

"I don't intend to be unreasonable about access to our son or daughter, Piper."

"Access?" she said, feeling completely dense.

"I don't expect to restrict your interaction with our child."

Oh, my God, she thought. *He's acting as if this is a done deal. As if I've said yes already, or worse, as if I have absolutely no choice in the matter.*

"Access won't be an issue," she said flatly.

"I'm pleased to hear you're prepared to be reasonable about this."

"I think you misunderstand me. Access won't be an issue because there won't *be* any access—there won't be any baby."

Rather than argue with her, Wade surprised her with a smile. A smile that held not an ounce of humor in the curve of his beautiful lips and which didn't so much as light his piercing eyes with a spark of warmth. Instead, it gave his face the look of a predator. One well used to winning.

Piper took another step back from him and crossed her arms instinctively.

"What are you smiling about? You can't make me change my mind. What you're suggesting…it's ridiculous. No, it's more than ridiculous. It's impossible!"

"Impossible? I think not." He hesitated a moment, his face settling into serious lines far more in keeping with the expression in his eyes. "Unless, of course, you're in a position to repay the money you owe me?"

His words hit her straight to her chest. Of course she wasn't able to repay him anything. She didn't even have enough money to stay in a hostel for a night. He had it all. Everything that had ever been hers and then some.

"You know damn well that I can't pay you back, you bastard. You have already taken everything that should have been mine." She flung her arms out. "This—my home, my history—not to mention my mother's art collection. You already own all that. You even had my father!"

As soon as she said the words she realized exactly where her pain and anger were centered. Her father. It was the final blow to know that he'd loved her so little that he'd sold everything to Wade. Every last thing in her world that had meant anything to her whatsoever.

"For what it's worth, I loved Rex like a father. At least I was there for him when he needed someone," Wade commented softly.

"I'd have been home if I'd known." Piper turned and faced out the window, speaking to the room rather than the man behind her who held the power to reshape her future. "I bet you even discouraged him from letting me know he was ill."

She felt, rather than heard, him close the distance between them. Felt the heat of his body pierce the cold that wrapped her in its solitary grasp. His touch on her shoulder was surprisingly gentle. The heartless businessman from a moment before seemed to have vanished, replaced by the devoted, fiercely protective man she'd fallen in love with years before. The man who'd always made her feel so safe and cherished.

"You probably won't believe me but I urged him to tell you. Especially when he knew he didn't have much longer. Rex was nothing if not stubborn. A trait you both shared." Even his voice was softer, more caring—and the wry fondness in his tone was so familiar that she felt the last wall around her heart crumble, setting all her emotions free.

The sob that been building in her chest escaped. After today's revelations and Wade's demand, she could no longer keep a lid on the anguish inside.

He turned her body and enveloped her in his arms, her

face against his chest. One hand, fingers splayed, rubbed big circles across her back. The other held her head gently against the rock hardness of his body.

It shouldn't feel so good, she told herself. She should pull away, refuse his offer of solace—he was the enemy—but instead, she found her fingers knotting in the fine cotton of his business shirt, felt the wrenching sobs that came from deep within her. Welcomed the warmth of his embrace.

Eventually she managed to bring herself under control, her sobs settling to the occasional snuffle. Beneath her hands she became aware of the tension that drew Wade's body as taut as a bow, felt his indrawn breath before he spoke.

"Would it be so bad, Piper? We were good together once."

His voice was pitched low, the coercion a subtle thread in his tone—compelling her to agree. Piper shook her head. Her tear-stained face leaving tracks of moisture in an untidy streak across the pristine whiteness of his business shirt.

"Please," she said, her voice strained and small as she drew away from the treacherous comfort of his arms. "Give me some time to work something out. At least give me time to think about what you're asking."

For a second she thought he'd refuse. That he'd press her for an immediate answer before either throwing her physically out the door or, alternatively, tossing her over his shoulder and taking her upstairs.

A zing of heat spiked through her core at the thought of the latter and she felt her empty womb clench tight in anticipation. Dammit, even her body was letting her down. It still remembered the way he used to make her feel, how good they'd been together. But that was all in the past now, she reminded herself. The man she'd loved had changed into someone she barely recognized. She couldn't love this stranger, and he certainly no longer loved her. It was all wrong to think of a child coming out of this. She could no more deny her intense physical attraction to him than she could stop breathing, but there was no way she was going to have another baby with him under these circumstances.

Another baby? Who was she kidding? She'd failed with the last one. Why would this time be any different? She couldn't go through that again. Wouldn't. Hadn't she lost enough already? Her fear must have shown on her face because Wade eventually gave her a short nod.

"You have until dinner tonight."

Four

Piper was too stunned to react to his words. She could only watch helplessly as Wade left the room. She heard him let himself out the front door and make his way down the front steps and across the crushed-shell-covered driveway to his car. The muted roar of his sleek gunmetal gray Porsche and the spray of shells signaled his departure and allowed her to release the breath she hadn't realized she held captive in her chest.

Her mind scattered on the monumental task ahead of her. She cast a quick glance at the antique carriage clock on the fireplace mantel. It was hard to believe it wasn't yet past midday. But that in itself was a bonus. At least it gave her time to see if she could raise the kind of money she was going to need to put Wade's appalling suggestion to bed.

To bed? What was she thinking? She rubbed at her face with both hands as if she could erase the thought once and for all.

She had to find some money from somewhere. Anywhere.

Banks were out of the question—she had no collateral to speak of. There was only one thing for it. She had to try to garner favor with her father's cronies. Surely someone, somewhere, would step up to help her.

Piper spun on her heel and stalked out of the room and across the hall to the library and settled at what had been her father's desk. Her hand shook slightly as she eased open the right-hand drawer to extract Rex's personal address book. She flipped open to the letter *A* and ran her finger down the list of names. It was a start. All she had to do was drum up the courage to actually make the requests.

The sun was waning in the autumn sky as she hung up the handset for the last time. Her ear ached from the amount of time she'd held the phone pressed to it, but nowhere near as much as her heart. It appeared that when she'd left, she'd burned all her bridges. Her perceived abandonment of her father had blacklisted her among every last person he'd called a friend. She hadn't been able to raise a single dollar.

She cast a glance at the untouched sandwich and cup of tea that Mrs. Dexter had brought to her a few hours ago. She hadn't felt like eating it then and she certainly didn't feel like it now. Just the thought of food was enough to tip her stomach, but that was nothing in comparison to what the concept of her rapidly diminishing alternatives gave her.

"Ah, lovey, you haven't eaten."

Mrs. Dexter bustled into the library and tutted her disapproval as she removed the tray from the corner of the desk.

"You won't get your bonny figure back if you don't take better care of yourself, Miss Piper."

"I'll be fine," Piper said quietly.

"Fine, humph! You'll be needing a bit of flesh on those bones of yours if you're going to attract the interest of a fine young man like Mr. Collins again."

Piper lifted her head and stared at Mrs. Dexter in horror.

"Why would I want to do that?" she couldn't help herself from asking.

"Why wouldn't you?" Mrs. Dexter gave her an uncharacteristically sly wink. "After all, it's not as if you're strangers to one another, is it?"

"I really don't think—"

"Oh, dear, listen to me. Here you are, only a day home and I'm already on at you. Why don't you go upstairs and get changed into something pretty for dinner. Mr. Collins will be home in an hour or so and I'm sure he'll be wanting you to look your lovely best. Although what we're going to do about that hair I just don't know."

"Mrs. Dexter!" Piper raised her voice, earning a look of chastisement from her old family retainer. "I'm sorry, Dexie," she amended, softening her tone. "It's been a while since I've had any looking after. I'm a bit rusty."

"Of course you are, lovey. But you're home now, where you belong. So why don't you run along and do as I said and when you're all finished, Dexter will serve drinks in the parlor before dinner."

It was all Piper could do to stop herself from shaking her head. She was twenty-eight years old, for goodness' sake, but in Dexie's mind she'd always be a little girl. Between the Dexters and her father, no wonder she'd never learned to grow up. That said, the prospect of taking a little distance from her failed attempts to raise *any* funds, let alone the kind of money she needed to clear her debt with Wade, did hold some appeal.

"Dexie, do we have any boxes in the house?"

"What? Storage boxes, you mean? Whatever do you want those for?"

"I'd like to clear some of the things from my room."

The older woman looked stricken. "Change your room?"

Piper forced a smile to her lips. "Yes, I'm not a little girl anymore, Dexie. I think it's time a whole lot of the things in there were packed up and moved away somewhere."

"But Mr. Mitchell—"

"Isn't with us anymore. And even if he was, I can't imagine he'd have any use for my old porcelain dolls. I don't mean to be harsh, but it really is time to move on."

Mrs. Dexter folded her lips in a straight line of disapproval and sniffed audibly.

"Well, if you insist. I'll see that Dexter brings some up for you, along with some packing foam and Bubble Wrap. We still have the boxes Mr. Collins brought when he moved in but I can't say I ever expected to see them used again so soon."

Piper held back the words she longed to say, words along the lines of wishing Mr. Collins would pack those boxes once more and move right back out again. Instead she opted for a civilized thank-you and made her way upstairs.

She quickly slipped into an old T-shirt and pair of sweatpants, the brand name imprinted across her buttocks in all its labeled glory. She shook her head. For what it had cost for both items, she could have fed a family in North Africa for a month, probably longer. The thought brought the enormity of the amount she owed Wade front and center in her mind again.

What the hell was she going to do?

An hour later she was no nearer to finding a solution but at least she'd had the chance to busy herself, and her mind, with clearing the shelves in her room of the remnants of her childhood. She'd individually wrapped the dolls in Bubble Wrap then laid layers of packing foam in between until each one was put away. As soon as all the glass-eyed empty faces were hidden behind the lids of the boxes, she felt something in her body begin to ease. As if she was no longer under constant scrutiny. No longer being held up in judgment against some impossible, unattainable ideal of perfection.

She stiffened as she heard the sound of a heavy measured tread outside her bedroom door. Clearly Wade was back from the office. No doubt he'd be changing and then returning downstairs for a predinner drink. The footsteps slowed before continuing along the landing toward his bedroom.

He'd expect an answer from her shortly and she still had no idea of what she was going to say.

What *could* she say? She had no means to pay him back, of which he was fully aware, which left her very little option for anything else. She was exactly where he wanted her. But why her? Why a baby?

She didn't believe for a minute that he didn't have time for a relationship. There were umpteen women who would happily have his child for the chance to have a piece of him, no matter how small. Was that what it was? Did he think the old animosity between them would stop her from being a problem? Prevent her from wanting a proper relationship with him?

A twinge deep inside reminded her how she'd destroyed the relationship they'd had through her petty selfishness, her unwillingness to share any part of his love. That had to be why he was prepared to offer her the deal he had. Deal? Who was she kidding? The word implied something reciprocal, but she still stood to be the loser even if she did agree to his outrageous suggestion.

So she wouldn't have a debt to him anymore. She certainly wouldn't have anything else, either. She'd be beholden to him for everything. Hell, she already was.

But what of the baby he said he wanted so very much? There was no doubt in her mind he would love his son or daughter with a single-minded devotion that only a parent could give. But would that excuse the lack of any kind of warmth or affection with which the child would be created? She couldn't help thinking back to her last pregnancy—to the child who had been conceived without conscious intention, and yet with so much deep, genuine passion.

Piper sat back on her bed and placed both her hands over her belly. The miscarriage of his baby had been one of the hardest things she'd ever had to go through in her life. When she'd first discovered she was pregnant, she'd considered coming home. Facing Wade with the truth that their lovemaking had given them both something they'd never dreamed they deserved. A child to love together.

But, in her mind, had been the bitter reminder that he'd chosen her father over her. That he'd made a conscious decision to further his career rather than be with the woman he'd said he loved. To her, back then, his decision had been all about putting her father and, most especially, his work before her. Something her father had always done all her life. It had been the final nail in the coffin that bore their dead relationship.

She'd finally resolved to go through the pregnancy alone. A decision that, in the end, proved futile when she'd suffered a miscarriage at fourteen weeks. Brokenhearted all over again, Piper had responded the same way she had every other time her hopes for love or happiness had fallen apart. She'd picked up her life anew. Partied hard, then partied harder still. No matter what she'd done, even though the hurt didn't show, the pain lingered inside her—and it was as fresh today as it was when she'd realized there was nothing she could do to prevent the infinite sense of loss. Their baby was gone—and Wade's rejection all those years ago meant that he still didn't even know she'd ever been pregnant.

Of course time and distance and even a little maturity had shown her that Wade had taken the right course. To have left his job back then would have been foolish in the extreme, and Wade was anything but foolish. It was why her father had taken him on in the first place—initially as an intern, then subsequently as a junior executive. She knew his loyalty to Rex Mitchell was absolute and came from a deep-seated respect and gratitude toward her father for taking a chance on him. And now look where he was. Head of the biggest export company in the country.

She'd been too young, too foolish and much too selfish to ever have been good for him back then. But what about now? While a part of her argued she should never have come back, logic also made a solid case that she'd needed to come home. Needed to finish healing. Needed to make amends for not being the daughter her father had wanted, for not being the woman Wade had needed. Maybe, just maybe, being that woman for him now.

Months ago as she'd cradled an undernourished toddler on a continent half a world away, she'd acknowledged how precious life was, how important the relationships within that life, and she'd promised herself she'd make it up to Rex and Wade, if they'd let her. That she could now never reconcile with her father was a cross she was going to have to bear the rest of her life. But Wade was another story.

Could she do what he'd asked of her in an attempt to make amends? The very thought sat uncomfortably with her. She'd be using a child, *their* child, as a tool to salve her own conscience. Everything inside her rebelled at the idea of being so manipulative—it was wrong on so many levels she couldn't even begin to count. Her arms still ached for the baby she'd never gotten to hold. Until that moment when she knew the tiny life inside her had died, she'd have entered into an agreement like Wade was suggesting without so much as blinking, if it got her financial freedom. She'd learned not to be that kind of person anymore. The past few years had taught her so very much about life, loss and even love.

Love. What if they stood a chance of reigniting their old relationship? Of building something worth saving and, this time, getting it right? The idea was both daunting and exhilarating at the same time and, for the first time since she'd arrived home and heard the news about her father, she felt as if she genuinely had a purpose again. It was a complete shot in the dark but she had no other alternatives to consider.

She glanced at her clock and noted she had better get ready for dinner. He expected her response and she didn't want to keep him waiting.

She got up off the bed and opened wide her wardrobe doors, seeking a dress that she knew had to still be here. It felt a little weird to know that her things had been maintained the whole time she'd been away but she pushed the thought aside. Her father had believed he'd been doing the right thing by her. Loving her in his way. It was a pity that she hadn't understood that at the time. She'd only been able to see that he hadn't loved her the way she'd wanted. For Piper, once she'd closed the front door behind her, all she'd wanted was distance. Her father had refused, yet again, to allow her to work within Mitchell Exports, in any capacity—telling her instead to do what she was good at, being beautiful and dressing well. In short, being a symbol of his success.

The response had been so typical of him. He had simply refused to believe she could be anything but ornamental. So she'd left home in defiance. Swearing she'd never come back until he'd see she was as strong and capable as any woman and asked her to return. She should have known better. Rex Mitchell asked nothing of anyone. If he couldn't make it happen by himself, it wasn't going to happen in his world. Wade was that way now, trapping her in a situation where he could force her to do what he wanted. Would she give in to his demand? She still wasn't entirely sure. She was scared at the thought of getting pregnant again, especially considering what had happened last time. But maybe this was her chance, as twisted as it seemed, to finally make things right. For her. For Wade. And for their baby.

Her hand finally settled on the dress she sought. Made

of dark blue and silver patterned silk, its lines were soft and flowing and would accommodate her more slender figure without looking too big on her.

If anything, she thought as she examined herself in the mirror a few minutes later, the dress looked even better on her now than it had the last time she'd worn it. The three-quarter sleeves showed off the tan she still bore on her arms, while the soft flowing lines of the skirt lent her a femininity she hadn't indulged in for far too long. She slid her feet into a pair of dangerously high-heeled silver pumps that picked out the threads of silver in the fabric of her gown and tied her dreadlocks back with a silver scarf.

She had no makeup with her, hadn't even worn any for several years now, so she was pretty much ready to join Wade downstairs. She hesitated at her bedroom door, her hand on the old-fashioned brass knob, her teeth worrying at her lower lip. What would she say to him? She couldn't simply capitulate to his wishes, no matter what. She certainly wasn't about to turn into a baby factory to salve his need to be a father. There had to be some ground rules. Some guidelines. What about custody? He'd said he would be reasonable about access but what was his idea of reasonable? And where would she and the baby live?

She tightened her fingers around the doorknob. She wouldn't be a pushover, even though he had her back against the wall over the money. There was no way she'd set up a child of hers to be a bargaining chip for the rest of its life. If he wanted them to have a baby together, there would be some conditions he'd have to agree to. Ultimately she had the power to say no. She could walk out that door tonight and find shelter somewhere until she could get back on her feet. Sure, things would be tough, but if he wasn't prepared to acquiesce on certain points then this plan of his was not happening. At least not with her.

* * *

Wade stared out over the subtly lit expansive emerald green lawn and tried to convince himself he wasn't nervous. He knew Piper was still upstairs, he'd heard her moving about in her room when he'd arrived home. She'd had ample time to come to her decision. But what would it be? She'd always been such a mercurial creature and he'd seen nothing in her that changed his mind on that score since her arrival home yesterday.

He took a sip of the sauvignon blanc in his glass. Had it really only been yesterday that she'd come back? She still had the capacity to turn his world upside down and inside out. He felt as if they'd gone several rounds against one another in the past twenty-four hours. In fact, as he'd clutched at sleep toward dawn this morning, he'd had to acknowledge a hard truth. Despite everything, she still had the ability to inveigle her way past his defenses. He'd thought he was completely over her, over what she had done to him—but he'd been so very wrong. She still had the capacity to hurt him and there was no way on this earth he was going to hand that back to her on a platter. He doubted his mentor would have approved of his tough love attitude. The older man would have been only too happy to see her arrive on the doorstep, and would have bent over backward to make things easy for her. Time had softened Rex's irritation with her for what he'd seen as nothing more than a temperamental spat.

"Look after her for me" had been Rex's dying words and, fool that Wade was, he'd promised. But Rex had said nothing about Wade putting in a few conditions of his own when it came to providing for Rex's prodigal daughter. She owed him far more than some trifling sum of money, and he *would* be repaid.

He wasn't oblivious to the fact that she might flat out say no to him and leave him to his own devices in attempting to recover the financial debt. But he was counting on the fact that she was enough of Rex's daughter to find an outstanding loan an anathema to her. There was also the slow burning spark of attraction that still simmered between them. She'd never been able to turn away from him before, he doubted she had the fortitude now. When Piper Mitchell wanted something, or someone, she'd usually do anything to get it. What she did after that was a little more obscure.

A sound at the door made him turn from the window. The sight of her was a visual punch to his solar plexus. He remembered the dress she was wearing in vivid detail. Remembered removing it from her body just as explicitly. Instantly his body grew rock hard at the memory of the indulgent and sybaritic night they'd spent together.

Piper's blue eyes met his across the room and in that instant he knew she'd chosen this dress on purpose. He bowed his head in a small nod of acknowledgment. He'd give her this point but it would be the only one she'd score tonight. He wasn't above conceding a strategic advantage here and there but it would be a brief concession, that much was certain.

"A glass of wine?" he offered, crossing the room to the sideboard.

"Thank you, that would be lovely."

Wade lifted the bottle of wine from the frosted silver cooler on the sideboard and poured a measure of the wheat-colored wine into a crystal goblet. He lifted the glass and took it over to where Piper had settled in one of the chairs.

"Had a busy day?" he inquired as she took the glass from his hand, painstakingly avoiding touching his fingers, he noted with some degree of satisfaction.

He rattled her on a physical level if not on an emotional one. Knowing that gave him an immense sense of satisfaction.

"You can quit with the pleasantries, Wade. We both know you couldn't care less what I did with my day."

"Now, that's not true. Not at all. I have it on good authority you were extremely busy this afternoon, making calls."

Piper stiffened in her chair. "You know?"

Wade shook his head deprecatingly. "I have to admit, I admire your resourcefulness, and your ability to stow away every last ounce of pride you once had, to have made those requests. It can't have been easy."

She took his veiled insult with surprisingly good grace.

"I learned that pride comes before a fall a long time ago. Thing is, have you?"

He laughed in response. "I never did let my pride get in the way of my success."

"Really? Maybe you should check yourself out again. Seems to me you have an inordinate amount of it now."

The smile stayed plastered on his face. She had no idea what he'd sacrificed to get where he was now. Beginning with her, in fact. But that was about to change.

"So did your calls elicit the response you wanted, Piper?" he asked as he sat down on the chair opposite hers.

"You obviously know exactly what kind of response I got. You can't tell me Dad's old friends weren't on the phone to you the instant they hung up with me."

"Actually, some of them were on the phone to me before you rang them," he conceded. "The rumor mill was busy this afternoon."

"And I suppose you told them not to lend me the money I need?"

There was a thread of steel in her voice that spoke of her frustration, but looking at her he'd never have guessed how angry she must have been to be thwarted in her attempts. Her expression remained serene, her eyes clear and bright. Even her lips were full and soft, not drawn into a line of tension as he'd have expected.

He shifted in his seat and tore his gaze from her mouth. His body still hadn't quite cooled down after that hit when she'd come into the room.

"Actually, I didn't have to. Your reputation preceded you."

His words scored a direct hit this time, he could see it in her eyes. He was suddenly sick of the game playing. He wanted to get right to the point of their meeting tonight.

"Have you reached a decision?" he asked.

"I thought you said I had until dinner," she replied, looking at the mantel clock with exaggerated interest.

"Don't beat around the bush, Piper. Will you or won't you have my child?"

Five

She rose from her chair in a fluid graceful movement. She always had the poise of a dancer, he remembered. Her limbs were supple and lithe…and there he went again. Hard, hot and wanting her. She strolled over to the deep sash windows and looked outside for a moment before turning to face him.

Her face was composed but he could see the anxiety in her eyes. Feel the tension that rolled off her in waves.

"I've been giving the matter some thought and it seems to me that I do not have all the facts I need to make a decision one way or the other. I have some questions," she said, lifting her chin ever so slightly in challenge.

"Ask away," he replied, holding his ground.

"If I were to agree to your proposal, there would need to be a written agreement between us. I don't trust you not to renege on your offer to expunge the debt you tricked me into."

Tricked her into? It wasn't worth arguing, so he let it go. "Okay, so you want a written agreement. What else?"

"How am I to support myself if I agree to have your baby?"

"By getting a job just like anyone else, I expect."

"So you don't think it would be your responsibility to provide for me?"

"You won't go hungry, Piper. Mrs. Dexter will make sure of that."

"You want me to stay here? Living under the same roof as you?"

"Until the baby's born, at least. That way I'll be sure you're taking the proper steps to look after our child prior to its birth. What you decide to do after that really doesn't interest me. If you choose to make your own home elsewhere, that's your prerogative."

"You'd let me take the baby and live away from here?" Incredulity made her voice rise.

"You misunderstand me. I said if *you* choose to make your home elsewhere. My child will stay here. He or she will be raised in this house, surrounded by their birthright."

"But the baby's care, feeding? What if I want to be a part of that?"

"You're saying you do?"

"I'm not confirming anything just yet."

"Piper, the baby will miss out on nothing. I will have nannies round-the-clock if necessary. Care will not be your responsibility."

She averted her head from him momentarily, but when she turned back her eyes were blazing.

"If I have a baby with you, you can be damn sure that its care will be my responsibility."

He shrugged, determined not to reveal his surprise at her latent maternal instinct coming to the fore. The prospect of her already being protective about a child who hadn't even been conceived was contradictory to what he knew about her and he found it unsettling. He hadn't expected her to be so... *feral*, about it, for want of a better word. Why now? Why this baby?

"Whatever you say. We can discuss that element further if you concede to my request."

"Request." She made a face, her mouth twisting in a line of disapproval. "As if you give me any real choice in the matter."

"You can still say no, Piper," he reminded her.

Her pride aside, he doubted she'd give up everything to live rough and fight her way in life starting from absolutely nothing.

"What if I want to stay here and be a part of my baby's life?"

"We could come to some arrangement."

"And what about payment?"

Ah, now we come to the truth, he thought. The real Piper Mitchell is in the building. "Money, to have our baby? Is wiping clean the sum you owe me not sufficient for you, Piper?"

"I'll need to buy things, for myself and for the baby. And if I do go ahead with this, I'd like to be under the care of a specialist."

"While you're under my roof, I will cover your medical costs."

"How generous of you," she said bitterly. "What if I choose not to live under your roof?"

"Not an option. As I said, I need to be able to ensure the baby's health and well-being until the point of delivery. After the baby is born, that would be your choice, of course. We would need to come to some arrangement regarding your visitation rights. Quite frankly, with your position, I don't see myself having any difficulty in gaining full custody, do you?"

"You're forcing me to stay here?"

"I didn't say that," he replied smoothly. "As I've said, once our baby is safely delivered you'll be free to leave whenever you like."

"How convenient for you. You expect me to walk away and never look back."

"It's what you do, isn't it?" he challenged softly.

She paled in response, uncharacteristically lost for words. Wade felt a sharp wave of regret for what he'd said, a wave he swiftly quashed. He couldn't afford to show any weakness. Not when so much hinged on her agreement.

"Is there anything else?" he asked.

"Yes, I want my mother's art collection back. It was her express wish that it be mine and it should have been mine all along."

He stood silent for a while, the seconds stretching out interminably between them. Of course she'd want the collection. He was well aware of Rex's concerns that she'd split it up to sell off individual paintings and then fritter the money away on her extravagant lifestyle. Still, it wasn't his place to say what she did with it.

"So let's get this right. Basically all you want from me is your mother's art collection, along with your outstanding debt being forgiven?"

"There's one more thing."

Of course there was. "What is it?"

"I want a job at Mitchell Exports."

A job? She was full of surprises today, wasn't she? he thought. Despite her very weak position, she could still make the kind of outrageous demands that had characterized the Piper he'd once known. A man had to admire her for her tenacity, he reluctantly admitted to himself.

"What would be the point in that? You're not trained in anything except spending money."

"I don't care what I get to do, but I deserve a place in that business. If you aren't prepared to find me work there, the deal is off."

"Minimum wage, then. I don't see why you should be paid

any more than that." He doubted she'd even be worth that much. "Do we have a deal?"

"If you give me a job we're certainly a step closer to coming to an agreement. I deserve a way to earn some money to support myself later on—why shouldn't I trade in on the family connection to the business?"

Wade momentarily struggled to control the exhilaration that swelled through him. They might be closer to an agreement, but at what cost? Her demand for a role at Mitchell Exports had thrown him somewhat, especially coupled with her uncharacteristic protectiveness toward a child they had yet to conceive. He had her right where he wanted her, yet at the same time he felt as if he was being manipulated, and that feeling put him very much on the defensive. He quelled the sudden rapid thrum that had lifted his pulse several notches—reminding himself that he didn't have her full agreement yet.

"If I agree to your terms, there are some of my own that I expect you to adhere to."

"Name them."

"First, I want you to undergo a full medical checkup. While you look healthy enough, given your lifestyle choices, I want a guarantee that you're fit to bear my child."

"My lifestyle choices?" she choked.

"Your antics in recent years have been cloaked from the media, unlike your behavior when you left here which was well documented in the tabloids. Who knows what you might have picked up?"

Two bright spots of color lit her cheeks. "What I might have picked up? And you? Where have you been finding *relief*? Might I ask the same of you? I have no desire to catch anything from you, I'm sure you understand."

Again, he found himself fighting to hide his admiration at her response. Here she was, most definitely the underdog, and yet she still didn't hold back, instead giving back as good as was dished out to her.

"In the interests of fairness, I have no objections to providing you with a clean bill of health. I'll make arrangements for us both in the morning."

Piper brushed past him and picked up her wine glass from the table and held it in the air in a bold salute. "Do we have a deal then?"

Wade covered the distance to where he'd left his glass and picked it up, touching the rim of the crystal to hers. "We do."

Piper fought to control the tremor that rippled through her body. She'd done it. She'd agreed. They were going to have a baby together. She didn't know whether to feel excited or simply terrified, although the latter fought for supremacy.

When would he want to begin the baby-making process? she wondered. Obviously at least not until they both had the all clear from the doctor. She'd felt so insulted, so dirty, when he'd made his stipulation. She had never been promiscuous. Sure, she'd partied along with the rest of them, but she'd never indiscriminately slept with other men. After the first two times she'd allowed anyone close enough to actually go to bed with them, once she'd left New Zealand behind, she knew that no man would ever compare to what she'd shared with Wade. It was simply easier to stop looking for it in every man she met, knowing that none of them ever had that special spark that was in constant evidence between her and the man standing opposite her right now.

As anxious as she was about their agreement, a tiny burst of excitement tinged with a healthy dose of apprehension began to unfurl from deep down inside. He'd changed in so many ways since they'd last been together. He was far more dominant now and appeared far harder than he'd been before, as if he tolerated nothing that tried to stand in his way—had he changed in other ways, too? Would he still be the caring and considerate lover she'd known, or had she irretrievably destroyed that person when she'd left him?

Would they make love, or would the conception of their baby be a clinical thing? Sex for the sake of it, or even conception achieved by artificial means? The sure knowledge that she would find out eventually was no consolation.

Piper realized with damning clarity that, as usual, she'd leaped into this thing without seriously thinking through all the consequences. Dread filled her belly. It was too late now. If she wanted to be taken seriously, she had to stand by her word. And, more than anything, she had to prove her worth—to herself and to Wade.

Later on she had no idea how she'd managed to get through dinner with Wade in the formal dining room. The table, which comfortably seated twelve, was spread with crisp white linen and glittering tableware and looked innocuous enough until you noted the place settings. One at the head of the table, the other intimately to its right.

While she had no doubt the food had been delicious, Dexie wouldn't have had it any other way, she could no sooner remember what it was she had eaten than she could say what it was they had talked about during the meal. It had been a time to be endured, while the reality of what she'd agreed to do sank in deeper and deeper.

Sleep was elusive that night, fractured with dreams that vividly included Wade in various states of undress. Beside her, beneath her, within her. She woke at dawn to the sound of rain beating against the windows, driven past the deep eaves of the upper balcony by a biting cold southwesterly wind. Overheated by her subconscious, she rose from her bed and pressed her face against the cool glass pane of her window, finding relief in the heat being drawn from her skin.

She was chilled to the bone by the time she crept back between the sheets of her bed and fell into yet another disturbed sleep, waking only when Mrs. Dexter knocked firmly at the door to tell her that Wade awaited her downstairs in the library. A quick glance at her clock confirmed that she'd slept far too late—it was ten o'clock already—and doing so had left her feeling groggy and out of sorts.

Piper grabbed her father's robe and wrapped it around her, and shoved her feet into a pair of slippers before going downstairs. The door to the library was closed and she hesitated, her fist raised and ready to knock at the ancient wooden surface, but then her usual streak of independence asserted itself and instead she reached for the handle, twisting it sharply and shoving the door open.

Wade sat at her father's desk—*his* desk now, she supposed. He looked up as she entered, a small frown appearing momentarily between his dark brows.

"Trouble sleeping last night?" he inquired, his voice cutting through the air with an astuteness that instantly rankled her.

Piper bit back the acerbic response that rose on her tongue, choosing instead to smile and to seat herself in the chair opposite his desk with as much grace as she could muster.

"I slept fine, thank you. And you?"

The shadows under his eyes matched her own but his response was a curt yes before he bent his head to flick through a sheaf of papers on his desk. Papers he then put in a folder and handed over to her.

"This is our agreement. Take some time today to read through it. Either of the Dexters will serve as an adequate witness, unless you'd prefer to use Mr. Chadwick. I can always see if he's available."

"He didn't draft up the agreement?"

"No, I used my own solicitor for that."

"You certainly didn't waste any time, did you?"

Wade leaned back in his chair and steepled his fingers. "Getting cold feet, Piper?"

Cold everything, if the truth were to be told. She'd thought it would be a good idea to show him how little he affected her by coming downstairs in such a state of dishabille but she should have taken the time to assume an armor of propriety at the very least. She felt at a complete disadvantage right now compared to his immaculate tailor-fitted suit, his cheeks smoothly shaven and his hair combed back off his face. The scent of his cologne, while not overpowering, tormented her with every inward breath. Spicy, exotic, alluring.

She straightened her shoulders and dragged in a deep breath before speaking. "No, not at all. We reached an agreement and I will honor that." If only to prove to you I *can* be honorable, she thought privately. "And when can I start at Mitchell Exports?"

She squirmed a little as Wade rose one eyebrow and cast an inquiring glance over her attire.

"You were expecting to start today?"

A tiny smile quirked at the corner of his mouth, as if she had presented herself in no less a state of readiness than he'd expected.

"Of course not. Tomorrow will be soon enough."

Piper allowed her gaze to meet his across the highly polished walnut desk. She wouldn't back down, not an inch. She could be honorable and still keep her pride, couldn't she? Somehow?

A surprising glow of approval shone in Wade's eyes, a glow that sent a spiraling warmth deep to her core. It shocked her to realize that his approval meant so much to her.

"Do you think you can be ready to come into the office with me at eight tomorrow?" he asked, tilting his head slightly to one side, the smile now spreading into a full grin. But it seemed less judgmental than before, as if he was teasing her instead of truly mocking her.

When he put that smile into action, he really was something else, she decided. She'd bet anyone—man, woman or child—would be putty in his hands in the face of it. Shamefully, she was no more immune to his charisma than anyone else.

"Of course."

"Excellent. And I assume you still remember how to drive a stick shift?"

If wrestling a bouncing jeep over potholed, unsealed roads was any claim to success, she figured she could cope with Auckland city traffic.

"I do," she replied.

"Your appointment for your physical is today, at eleven. It might pay for you to change before you go." A teasing smile played around his lips. "Here's the address."

He flicked a card across the desk toward her. She lifted it up and saw the name of a private medical clinic tastefully printed across the top of the plain white card. A doctor's name beneath it in black script. A female doctor, she noted.

"Thank you. Is that everything?"

"For now."

He reached into his jacket pocket and pulled out a key ring and offered it to her. Piper stood and reached for the keys, but started as his fingers closed around hers as she went to remove them from his palm.

"My keys. Drive safely, okay?"

"I didn't know you cared," she said as flippantly as she could manage even as her heart began to race at his touch.

"You will be having my baby, of course I care."

The words hurt her far more than she'd expected. She knew she was a vessel for him to have that which he most wanted, but it shocked her to acknowledge that she wanted to be so very much more than that.

"Don't worry, I won't do anything to jeopardize the merchandise," she said, aiming again for lightness but knowing she fell short when he didn't release her hand straight away.

"I can always arrange a driver for you if you'd rather," he said.

"No, I'll be fine. Seriously. And you'd best let me go if you want me to be on time."

She looked pointedly at their hands and snatched hers, and the keys, away the second he released her.

"I'll see you this evening then?" she said, heading toward the door.

"No, I have an appointment this evening."

She stopped and turned back to face him. "Oh, a hot date?"

"Something like that," he replied.

He still planned to go on seeing other women, even as he got her pregnant?

"I thought you didn't have time for relationships," she pushed. It was like pressing on a bruise. You knew, no matter what, it was going to hurt.

"This definitely doesn't fall into that category." He smiled again.

"Oh, so it's just sex then?"

Oh, God. When would she learn to haul back on her runaway tongue?

This time he laughed out loud. "Would that bother you, Piper?"

It did bother her. Far more than she was prepared to admit to *him*.

"Well, in the interest of keeping clean, maybe it should," she challenged. "When is *your* appointment with the doctor?"

"Don't worry, there'll be no chance of me catching anything tonight that you should be worried about."

She sniffed audibly. "I should think not."

Then, with as much decorum as she could muster, she headed through the door. She was at the foot of the staircase when she heard his voice behind her.

"Piper, you could come with me if you want to."

"To spend an evening with one of your women? I don't think so."

She had some pride left.

He shrugged at her response. "No problem. I just thought I'd give you the option."

The option. She clutched the folder containing their agreement to her chest and fought not to laugh out loud. Options were in scarce supply for her these days.

"It's okay. I want an early night before starting work tomorrow, anyway."

"Your choice," Wade said as he turned and went back into the library.

For a moment Piper was tempted to follow him back in there. To tell him that she'd changed her mind. She knew it would eat her up all evening, knowing he was with another woman. Wondering whether he was kissing her, whether his hands would push aside her clothing to bare her skin to his touch. Whether her hands were touching him.

She shook her head fiercely. She had to stop torturing herself this way. But even as she ascended the stairs she knew there'd be one amendment to their agreement that he may not be too happy about, and that was going to be an exclusivity clause.

Six

Piper swiftly discovered that driving Wade's Porsche 911 Carrera GTS was a world away from the rackety old jeep she'd driven last month. Her hands settled on the three-spoke steering wheel, the covering of which felt like suede beneath her touch, and she took a deep breath before letting the engine roar to throbbing life.

Man, this car was like a hard-on with wheels. No wonder men loved things like this so much, she smiled to herself as she slowly cruised down the crushed shell driveway and out through the iron gates of the property. It seemed almost criminal not to detour to the nearest motorway and let the car show its paces, but she wasn't that flippant devil-may-care individual anymore.

The car handled like a dream and by the time she pulled into the designated patient parking at the health center she almost wished she had escaped into the countryside. Nerves assailed her. What if the checkup disclosed something that would jeopardize her agreement with Wade? She sucked in a deep breath and let it go slowly. She just had to get out of the car and visit the doctor and see for herself.

The clinic's rooms were spacious and elegantly furnished. A far cry from what she'd become used to during her volunteer work abroad. She doubted a fly or a speck of dust would so much as dare to enter here. After giving her name to the receptionist, she sat in one of the comfortable waiting chairs and listlessly flicked through a magazine. She hadn't been there long before she heard her name called.

A woman, a little older than herself, stood waiting for her with a smile. As Piper approached, the woman thrust out her hand.

"Hi, I'm May Ritter. Wade asked if I could see you today."

So he was on first-name terms with the doctor? Piper gave her a surreptitious once-over as she shook hands and smiled in response. The woman was definitely attractive, with well-tamed, deep red hair, and a clear complexion any supermodel would die for. Bright green eyes sparkled behind frameless lenses.

"Come on through," May said.

She led the way down a short corridor and into a treatment room and gestured that Piper take a seat beside the desk that was pushed up against the wall.

"Now, tell me a bit about yourself," the doctor said, settling comfortably in the chair behind the desk and angling the computer screen toward her.

"What do you need to know?" Piper hedged. Where should she begin? The reality that she was here for a pre-pregnancy health check was all too real.

"Let's start with your full name, age and stuff like that, then we'll go into your medical history."

Piper felt a cold chill run down her back. Her medical history? That would mean disclosing her previous miscarriage. There was no way on this earth that she ever wanted Wade to find out about that. It wouldn't take much for him to put two and two together and realize that she'd been carrying his baby. And that she'd lost it.

"This information remains confidential, doesn't it?" she asked, her voice a little pitchy.

"Definitely. Wade wanted me to make sure you're in good shape to start a family, but any details you tell me will stay entirely between us. Wade's a friend, but that doesn't trump doctor-patient confidentiality."

"You know Wade personally?"

Could this get any worse?

"Oh, yes. He and my husband have been friends for about five years now. They have this ridiculous competitive thing going between them over weekly squash games. You'd think they'd have known each other a lifetime they're so close. Wade's the godfather of our three-year-old daughter. In fact, he's even babysitting for us tonight. Hopefully, part of my thank-you to him will be giving you a clean bill of health."

Ah, thought Piper, so that was his reason for not being home tonight. No wonder he'd looked so amused at her reaction. A flush of anger and embarrassment heated her cheeks. Why couldn't he simply have told her the truth rather than let her think he was seeing another woman? She dragged her attention back to the matters at hand.

Piper nodded. "All he needs to know is that I don't have any communicable diseases and that I'm healthy, right?"

"Sure, once we've run all our tests, etc., that's all he needs to know."

"Well, obviously I need to tell you this won't be my first pregnancy. Eight years ago I lost a baby at fourteen weeks." Piper swallowed against the lump that formed in her throat.

"I'm sorry to hear that. Were there complications with the pregnancy?"

Piper shook her head. "Just one of those things, they said."

May got up from her seat and sat in the chair next to Piper, taking one of Piper's hands in hers. "I'm sorry, Piper. It's never easy losing a baby, especially when there is no apparent reason. Did you have support at the time?"

"I was on my own. Aside from the medical staff, no one else knew."

May's fingers closed more tightly around Piper's in silent support. "That can't have been easy."

Piper blinked back the tears that burned in her eyes. "It wasn't. It makes me scared about this, though. About doing it again. What if—"

"Piper, there is probably no reason why you shouldn't have a perfectly normal pregnancy. That's why you're here today."

Piper nodded. "There's one other thing," she continued. "I've been working overseas for the past few years, volunteering with aid organizations. I contracted malaria a while back."

May reached across her desk for the folder in which she'd been making notes before and made a few notations. "How far back?" she asked.

"Just under four years ago."

"Any recurrences?"

"Not so far."

"Okay," May said, making a few more notes. "What sort of work were you doing?"

"Grunt work, for the most part. I'm not skilled in anything but you don't need a degree to help where it's needed. I basically just did what I was directed to do. Sometimes it was handing out food, other times holding an infant whose mother had just passed away."

"It sounds like heartbreaking work."

"It was at times, but at least I felt I could make a difference."

"I can see why that would have been important to you. Right," May said, standing up and putting her pen and folder back on the desk. "Let's get you up on the examination table and check you over."

To Piper's relief the rest of her check went smoothly,

inasmuch as something so intimate could go smoothly. May remained efficient and professional as she examined her thoroughly, occasionally asking questions and making notes as she went. She printed off a lab request and gave it to Piper.

"Take this through to the lab so we can complete these tests and then you're all done. I'll give you a script for some prenatal vitamins and folate. As soon as you've had the blood and urine tests done, you can fill the prescription and start taking them."

"So you don't see any problems with me falling pregnant fairly quickly?" Piper asked.

"Every case is different, but you've been pregnant before and there really isn't any reason why you should have any worries this time around. The only thing that could be a concern is the malaria. Should you relapse while you're pregnant, it could make treatment difficult and cause problems for the baby."

Piper swallowed. She'd contracted the illness in Africa, early on in her volunteer work. It was her own fault in blithely ignoring the warnings and not keeping her antimalaria routine up-to-date. The wake-up call had been a harsh one. She'd been fortunate not to experience a severe relapse since, but there were no guarantees she'd continue to be so lucky.

"Problems?"

"Many of the drugs used in the treatment of malaria are contraindicated during pregnancy. Have you experienced a relapse since your infection?"

"No, I haven't."

"Then let's hope that continues, hmm? We'll monitor you carefully, though."

May continued on with some further instructions for Piper on maintaining a healthy lifestyle. By the time Piper found herself back in the car park, her newly filled prescription clutched in one hand, Wade's car key in the other, her head was spinning. What had she let herself in for? The ramifications of what she'd agreed to were suddenly all too real and with that reality, fear of failure stole anew into her heart.

During the drive back home she considered their agreement in-depth. This was a monumental thing she had consented to. She had to make sure that this worked, for everyone's sake, but most importantly, for that of their child.

Wade let himself in through the front door later that night and heaved a sigh of relief to be home. As cute as May and Paul's daughter Maggie was, a whole evening with her was enough to wear out the hardiest of men. She was going to be a heartbreaker when she grew up, though, that was for sure. A feeling of intense protectiveness swamped him—as if he'd ever let anyone near enough to Maggie for her to break their heart.

It worried him sometimes, this fierce need to protect a child who wasn't even his. If he was this bad now, how would he feel about his own? He knew, better than most, how hardy children were. How they needed to push boundaries and find their paths in the world. But right now the idea of wrapping little Maggie in cotton wool and tucking her away somewhere safe for the rest of her life was inordinately appealing.

He couldn't wait to be a father. His own had been no role model and he was determined to prove that he could not only be more successful than the man who'd refused to continue to raise him, but he would be a far, far better parent. No child of his would ever be discarded. Not for any reason.

He cast a glance upstairs. From here he could see the door to Piper's room. The landing was dark with not so much as a glimmer of light from beneath her bedroom door. He was relieved she was in bed already—goodness knew every interaction they'd had so far had been fraught and contentious. After the day he'd had in the office where nothing had seemed to go right, and the evening with Maggie, who'd been way more demanding than usual, he was in no mood to go another round with Piper.

He turned toward the library so he could put his briefcase and laptop by the desk for an early start in the morning. As he opened the door he was surprised to see a movement in the darkened room. Only a slight glow from the fireplace lent illumination, casting a golden light across the very last person he wanted to see right now. She was dressed much as she'd been this morning, in her nightgown and her father's robe. Except the robe had fallen open as she'd dozed with her feet drawn up under her on the wingback chair, revealing smooth tanned skin and the slight swell of one breast exposed by the open buttons of her pristine white cotton nightgown.

She must have sensed him in the room because she shifted in the chair, her eyes opening, searching for him. "Wade?"

She sounded drugged with sleep.

"You were expecting someone else?" he countered, dryly.

And just like that she was wide awake. "Don't be ridiculous. I wanted to talk to you about the agreement. There's an addition I've made."

"An addition?"

When was she going to understand that she really didn't call the shots in this situation? He shook his head wearily.

"Piper, the agreement was drawn up in accordance with our earlier discussion—including your specific conditions. You cannot keep on amending it."

"It's just one change."

"Well, spit it out."

"I'd rather you read it, actually."

Piper walked over to his desk and picked up the folder she'd obviously put there. She opened it and took out the agreement, flicking through the pages until she found what she was looking for. He reached across the desk and flipped on the lamp, the sudden illumination revealing just how sheer the cotton of her nightgown was and how exquisitely shaped her nipples were as they pressed against the fabric.

His mouth dried and, if he hadn't known better, he would have thought all the blood in his body had just headed south. Wade tore his gaze from her and forced himself to accept the document. He leaned down over the desk, fighting his awareness of her standing next to him, desperately trying to ignore the alluring shadows of her form. As if she was aware of the torture she was putting him through, she grabbed the edges of her robe and wrapped them tightly across her body, tying the sash firmly at her slender waist.

Wade felt a momentary tug of regret before forcing his mind to the matter at hand. Her closely formed handwritten notes used clear and succinct language. *Very* clear and succinct language, he thought with an inner smile. So she didn't want him seeing other women. Given her response this morning it shouldn't surprise him. She'd been prickly when she'd thought he had a booty call rather than a babysitting assignment.

Knowing she was jealous of his other women was strangely satisfying, but the knowledge was, at the same time, a little unsettling. How did he really feel about that? Did he honestly want to pursue an exclusive relationship with Piper? Relationship should be the wrong word, but just the thought of it was enough to fill his chest with an unexpected warmth. He quelled the feeling almost immediately. This was Piper Mitchell he was talking about. He'd learned his lesson once, the hard way. He wasn't masochistic enough to involve his emotions with her again.

He straightened from the desk abruptly. Piper took a step back in reaction.

"Is that all?" he asked quietly.

She looked startled. Had she expected him to argue with her? To refuse to sign? Did she have no concept of what this child meant to him? Or how important it was that he regain from her what she'd taken? He'd have all but signed away his soul to get what should have been rightfully his all along.

"Y-yes," she stammered.

"Fine, I'll get my PA to witness my signature at work tomorrow and we can get down to business."

Even in the muted light he could see how she'd paled at his words.

"Business?"

"Yes, Piper," he said, stepping closer to her. So close he could see moisture glisten on her lips where she'd nervously swiped them with her tongue. "The business of making a baby."

She swallowed, dragging his attention from her lips to the long graceful sweep of her neck.

"Right. But we'll have to wait for the health check results to come back first, won't we?"

"Piper, seriously, if I didn't know you better I'd think you were nervous."

She swallowed again. "No, I'm not nervous exactly. I was just thinking today that we hadn't really gone into the mechanics of how we were going to create this child."

"Mechanics?" He smiled. "Well, it's been a while but I'm assuming people still do it the same way they have always done. You know—"

"So you don't want to go for artificial methods?" she interrupted.

Her voice had pitched even higher. She sounded a little scared. Such a change from the fearless girl he remembered. He was starting to feel bad about winding her up so much. It had always been so good between them, why would she be scared of that? Maybe she needed a reminder.

"Now, why would I want to do that, when we can enjoy this," he replied.

He reached forward, cupping one hand at the back of her neck and drawing her toward him. He bent his head, catching a glimpse of shock in her eyes before his lips captured hers. Her eyelids fluttered closed as he traced the seam of her mouth with his tongue, her lips parting on a gentle sigh. He deepened the kiss, pressing home his advantage and trying not to remember the last time he'd touched her like this. The last time he'd wanted her like this—with a force that threatened to consume him.

He swept his tongue along her lower lip before suckling it between his teeth, scraping softly on the tender membrane before releasing it again. Her body sank into his, the softness of her breasts crushing against his chest. The curve of her hips, her mound, aligning with his painfully hard erection. He craved her with a need he'd thought long suppressed. Wanted nothing more than to sweep the contents of his desk to the floor and to take her on that hard polished surface— to push up her nightgown over her waist and to sink between her glorious long legs, to her inner heat where he could lose himself, lose this overwhelming burning desire.

But, with a control borne of years of practice, he reined himself back, focused instead on nothing but their kiss, on inciting her to want him as much as he most definitely wanted her. Because when he took her to his bed, he wanted her to be a full and willing partner—physically at least. He would settle for nothing less.

Seven

Piper struggled to gather her thoughts, but they spun out of reach until she could only feel. Wade's kiss was a mastery of seduction. His lips a tantalizing tease across her own. His tongue a hot wet rasp of torment. She wanted more than this, more than a kiss. She wanted to feel his mouth on her body— her breasts, her belly, lower.

She squeezed her thighs tightly together against the swell of longing that ached at her core and wrapped her arms around his neck so she could press even more firmly against his length. His body felt different from how he'd been before. More heavily muscled through his torso, his legs stronger. But one thing remained the same. She recognized the feel and shape of a specific part of him as if it were only yesterday.

She trailed one hand down his chest, to the waistband of his trousers where she fumbled with his leather belt, desperate to test the weight and size of him in her hand. To feel his silken hardness, skin to skin.

He groaned into her mouth as her fingers pushed past

the elastic of his briefs and brushed the head of his penis. His erection jumped against her palm before she closed her fingers around his width and stroked. She felt the shudder go through him, heard him groan again as he tore his mouth from hers and fastened it anew in the curve of her neck.

And then the firm grip of his hand was at her wrist, gently pulling her away from him. Pushing her away from him. She fought to control her breathing, to get some semblance of control over her wayward behavior. Her body felt heavy, lethargic—aching with longing.

Her reaction to him—to the feel, the taste, the sheer craving she had for him—made her realize something that she hadn't wanted to consider in a very long time. She still had feelings for him—very deep feelings. The thought was a sobering wake-up call. That Wade desired her, she had no doubt. She'd felt the throbbing heat of his passion in her own hand only seconds ago. But could she hope that his feelings for her would ever again be more than the disdain he'd so clearly expressed?

She took a step away from him on legs that felt about as substantial as threads of cotton. Piper looked up to Wade's face. The light from the desk lamp cast shadows across his features. For a split second she thought she'd glimpsed something there, something from when she knew she'd held his heart in her hands as he had held hers. Before she'd systematically destroyed everything they'd had between them without realizing how much she would ultimately hurt them both. But that glimpse gave her a tiny shred of hope. Maybe they could make this work. Maybe, just maybe, they could build something new out of the ashes of their old relationship.

"I think we've proved we won't have any trouble on the compatibility score, don't you?" he said.

And there it was, back in full Antarctic chill. That aloofness that told her that while she might be able to affect him on a physical level, there was no way he was going to let her back inside on an emotional one.

She nodded, lost for a response.

"So there'll be no more talk about artificial conception?" he pressed.

She shook her head.

"Then I think you'd better get off to bed, don't you? You have a long day tomorrow at the office to look forward to."

Finally, she found her tongue. "Will we travel in together?"

"No, I need to be in early. I'll leave the car for you if you like."

"Or I could use Dad's," she said.

"Rex's Daimler was sold last year. There's the hatchback the Dexters use but they'll probably be busy with it tomorrow. What's the matter, didn't you like driving the Porsche? I can easily book a driver to take me into work."

She shook her head again. "That's not the point. What will everyone think if I turn up in your car? They'll assume the only reason I got a job there is because I'm sleeping with you."

He gave her a piercing look. "And that bothers you, that people might think—" he reached a hand out to trace her cheekbone "—we're on intimate terms?"

She jerked her head back but it did nothing to stop the tingling awareness on her skin.

"Yes, it bothers me. I meant what I said about learning to work there from the ground up. I need to learn to stand on my own two feet. I don't want any dispensations just because of who I am."

He chuckled but the sound lacked humor, and made the fine hairs on the back of her neck prickle in reaction.

"No dispensations like walking in off the street to a job even though you have no experience and no qualifications? Why does that not surprise me?" He rubbed his eyes with one hand. "Go to bed, Piper. I'll make sure you have sufficient means to get to work tomorrow. Means that ensure no one will think any the worse of you, I promise."

"Thank you," she said stiffly. "Good night."

"It's night all right," she heard him mutter as she walked past him and out the door. "Not that there's anything good about it."

Piper woke the next morning to the sound of Wade's car purring down the driveway. She stretched and rolled over to look at her clock. 6:00 a.m. He certainly wasn't kidding about heading to the office early. She rolled back into her previous position, seeking oblivion for perhaps another half hour, but the moment was gone. She couldn't get back to sleep. She was starting work today and the prospect thrilled and terrified her in equal proportions. What if she made a total fool of herself? What if everyone hated her when they found out she was Rex Mitchell's daughter? Would anyone still remember her or her reputation?

There were so many "what ifs" her head started to spin. She pushed aside her bed covers and flicked on the overhead light. Her eyes caught on the clothes she finally decided to wear for work. A plain pair of tailored navy trousers, teamed with a cream-colored blouse and a matching camisole underneath. She really needed to do something about getting some new bras, she thought. She couldn't go braless forever. She'd considered, again, the idea of padding up one of the bras in her drawer with tissue paper but had discarded it as quickly. She didn't want any other worries to occupy her mind while she started to learn the ropes of this next stage in her life.

Piper gathered her things and went through to her bathroom, a bubble of excitement beginning to form in her belly. She was starting work, paid employment, for the very first time in her life.

She stopped and looked at her reflection in the mirror. She'd changed so much since she had left here. Reinventing herself several times over from capricious daughter to single party girl to tireless aid volunteer. Now she was on the cusp of reinventing herself again.

She found exactly what she was looking for in the bottom drawer of her bathroom vanity. The scissors weren't unwieldy, but they weren't exactly the compact fine-precision steel of a hairdresser's instrument, either. Well, they'd have to do, she thought as she reached behind her and grabbed a dreadlock firmly in one hand. A swell of nausea rose from the pit of her stomach as she positioned the scissors and closed her eyes. Snip. There it was. The first real step toward the new Piper Mitchell.

By the time she stepped in the shower cubicle of the bathroom, she already felt different. Lighter. She laughed out loud. Of course she felt lighter. At least five years' hair growth lay scattered on the bathroom tiles. She lifted a hand to her head, feeling the wisps of hair that now clouded in a pale golden halo. She'd have to get it professionally shaped once she had some money but for now it would have to do.

After her shower she blow-dried her hair, combing her fingers through the unaccustomed short lengths. For someone who'd had long hair all her life it felt drastically different. She didn't doubt she'd get used to it, though. There, she was done. She stepped back and looked at herself in the full-length mirror on the back of the bathroom door.

Piper eyed herself critically. The new hair was certainly different, she decided, the makeup not too bad, and the overall effect with her clothes gave her what she hoped was a smart professional finish. Going back into her bedroom she took another look at her clock. Good heavens! She'd spent the better part of an hour and a half getting ready, it was almost seven-thirty. She'd better hurry or she'd be late for her first day and she couldn't bear to see the censure or, no doubt, the satisfaction on Wade's face if she wasn't there by start of business at half past eight.

Mrs. Dexter was in the kitchen when she arrived downstairs.

"Oh, my, what have you done to your hair?" she cried.

"Do you like it?" Piper asked, putting up a hand to touch her hair.

"Well, it beats what you arrived home with. I imagine it'll grow out soon enough. You always did have lovely hair. By the way, you'll be needing a raincoat," the woman remarked as she put a plate of scrambled eggs in front of a place setting on the kitchen table.

"Thanks for breakfast," Piper said, picking up a fork and sampling a mouthful before Mrs. Dexter's words sank in. "A raincoat? Whatever for?"

Mrs. Dexter pointed to a couple sheets of paper and a stack of coins on the table next to Piper's place setting. Piper slid the note out from under the coins. It didn't take long to read.

Here's the bus timetable. The nearest stop is about 800 meters from the house. Enjoy the ride.—W. P.S. I'll instruct the pay office to deduct the bus fare from your wages.

Piper almost laughed. The bus? Did he really think she'd shy away from catching the bus? Mrs. Dexter did, too, by the look of her. They had no way of knowing she'd traveled on far worse than Auckland's transport system. She carefully put the note on the table and lifted the timetable. She'd really have to hurry if she was going to reach the office on time. With little care for finesse, Piper shoveled down the last of the eggs and swiftly drank the coffee Mrs. Dexter had poured for her.

She rose from the table and put her dirty dishes in the sink then gave the older woman a smacking kiss on the cheek.

"Thanks, Dexie. I've got to go."

"Are you sure you'll be all right catching the bus?"

"I'll be fine, don't worry about me."

"You'll find a coat in the hall cupboard, and an umbrella."

"Perfect, thank you!" Piper cried as she raced upstairs to brush her teeth before leaving.

She knew what Wade was up to and she wouldn't give him the satisfaction of beating her down. Not now, not ever. She might have agreed to have his baby but there was no way he was going to call all her shots.

Wade walked to the reception area on the dot of eight-thirty.

"Any sign of Miss Mitchell?" he asked the receptionist.

"Oh, yes, sir. She's been here for ten minutes. Jane is showing her around, as you asked."

She was early? He hadn't expected that. No, to be completely honest, what he'd expected was a tantrum over the phone that he'd expected her to take public transport. The Piper he'd known would never have dreamed of such a thing. Still, he probably hadn't given enough consideration to the steel vein of stubbornness that ran down her spine.

"Thanks, I'll go find them."

"They're probably in accounts," the receptionist offered far too cheerfully.

Wade tried to keep his bewilderment in check as he headed toward the accounts department. He'd wanted Piper to start there, as a junior. If anything would break her ridiculous desire to work here, that would. He had no doubt she'd never so much as balanced a checkbook. Invoicing would definitely be her undoing. At least, he expected so.

He heard laughter as he walked down the corridor, not an uncommon sound in his workplace—he prided himself on the atmosphere he and Rex had built here—but this was more than usual. He entered the accounts department and saw a crowd of staff around one desk.

At the computer terminal a young woman sat with her back to him. Who, he wondered, before his body instinctively recognized what his own eyes had not. Piper. A very different Piper than the one he had kissed last night. What had she done to her hair? It had transformed into a short choppy multilayered cut. Far shorter than he'd ever seen her wear before. It emphasized the slenderness of her neck and the delicate line of her throat.

The laughter and bonhomie he'd heard suddenly fell silent. Piper looked over her shoulder from what she'd been doing. Her eyes locked onto him for a startled moment before dropping. He had the brief satisfaction of seeing a flush rise in her cheeks before she turned away.

"Everything under control?" he asked, irked to feel as if he was an intruder in his own firm.

"We're doing fine." Jane separated herself from the group and gave him a smile. "I think Piper will fit in extremely well here."

"That's good," he said, feeling completely the opposite. He looked around at the assembled group of staff. "But does it really take all of you to train her?"

One by one people muttered something and peeled back to their work stations, leaving just Piper and Jane with him. Jane gave him a speculative look. She'd worked here at Mitchell Exports the past five years and knew him well. She'd certainly never seen him speak to his staff like that before. The knowledge he was behaving unreasonably made him even more irritated.

"I'm glad to see you managed to get in on time, Piper," he said, gleaning a kernel of satisfaction as he saw her ears turn a little pink as his comment sank in.

"Did you think I might have a problem—" she hesitated a moment before adding "—sir?"

Well, that was telling him, wasn't it? He acknowledged her barb with a small, grim smile.

"Proof will be in your consistency, and your performance. It's not a popularity contest, you know."

"I'm aware of that, sir."

"And we don't stand on ceremony here, Piper. Just call me Wade."

She smiled back at him. The silence stretched out between them, with Jane standing at his side looking from one to the other as if she was at a tennis match.

"Well," he said uncomfortably, "I'd better not keep you from your work."

Piper merely continued to smile. He gave Jane a sideways look which wiped the smile from her face, then he turned and stalked out. Damn if she hadn't held the upper hand there all the way.

Once in his office he began to calm down, seeing his behavior for the ridiculous stunt it was. Were his expectations of her really so mistaken? Had she truly changed? He thought again about the bus ride she'd endured to get here on time, and the effort she'd obviously made to change her appearance and to fit in. He'd been unfair, he had to admit. She'd stepped up to the plate without so much as a murmur, and he at least owed it to her to acknowledge that.

He couldn't fault her. Not in anything she'd done so far today. With a sigh of resignation he reached across his desk and picked up the phone, dialing from memory the number of his car dealer. Some points were best made by gesture, he decided.

Piper gingerly walked up the driveway toward the house. As hard as her feet had become in the work boots or runners she'd habitually worn the past few years, spending a day in high heels was something she'd happily forgotten. The balls of her feet were almost raw, she was sure of it. Her first paycheck would have to go toward a sensible pair of shoes, she thought. The Piper she used to be would never have dreamed of doing such a thing, but she was most definitely more practical now. And if she was to bus to and from work each day, with the walks from the house to the bus stop and again at the other end to the office, then doing it all in reverse order each day, she'd need something sensible on her feet just to survive.

Huh, and she'd thought relief work was tough. While it had been demanding physically and emotionally, it had never left her this mentally exhausted. She certainly hoped that Wade wasn't planning on any more verbal rounds because she really wasn't up to it.

She lifted her head as she approached the house. Oh, great, she thought, noting a different car parked in the driveway. Visitors. She certainly hoped she wasn't expected to make an appearance. All she wanted to do right now was take off her shoes and give her feet a soak.

Piper veered along the pathway that led toward the back entrance of the house, hoping that she could avoid Wade and whoever he might be entertaining. But her hopes were dashed as she heard the big wooden front door swing open and Wade called her name as he stepped onto the wide veranda.

She stopped in her tracks and looked at him as he walked toward her.

"I owe you an apology," he said, the words stunning her with their simplicity.

"You were a jerk this morning," she replied stiffly. "I accept your apology."

She turned and started to walk away but his large warm hand settled on her arm and halted her in her tracks.

"Which part of this morning, particularly?" he asked.

She paused before answering, pretending to give the matter consideration. "Oh, pretty much all of it really," she finally replied.

He laughed, a genuine laugh that made his eyes crinkle at the corners and shaved years off his face.

"Well, that's telling me."

"Is that all you wanted?" Piper said, pointedly looking at his hand which still lay warm and heavy on her arm.

"Actually, no." With his spare hand he reached into his trouser pocket and withdrew a set of keys. "These are for you."

She avoided taking them from him. "What are they for?"

He nodded at the car parked in the driveway. "That. It's yours."

Inside she silently rejoiced and her feet agreed with her. A car. It would give her the independence and the degree of separation she needed, while removing the inconvenience of having to catch the bus—especially on days like today when it had been raining on and off. But she didn't want him to think she was asking for a handout. If she had to take public transportation every day from now until kingdom come to prove herself to him, then that was what she'd do. She lifted her chin and looked him straight in the eye. "What's wrong with the bus?"

"I thought you might prefer the comfort of a car of your own. Especially once you're pregnant."

The words brought home the reality of their situation to her with sudden clarity. Up until now it had all been a war of words, but hearing him say it made it a great deal more real.

"And will you deduct its value from my wages, too?" she said, fighting for some measure of control.

His mouth quirked on one side in that half smile he was inclined to do around her these days. "No, I won't. It's a gift. There's an account for you at the local gas station, too."

"Thank you," she said simply, accepting the keys from his hands and going to look at the car.

It wasn't the newest vehicle on the block but it certainly wasn't the oldest, either.

"I didn't think you'd want anything showy or expensive," Wade said from right behind her.

"I appreciate it. After your performance this morning, Jane's already looking at me funny."

"She'll get over it." Wade shrugged. "Want to take it for a spin around the block?"

Piper thought for a moment of the soak she wanted to give her feet but the temptation to see how the car felt to drive was too tempting.

"Sure, you coming?"

In answer he opened the passenger door of the car and slipped inside, securing his seat belt. "Well, come on," he urged.

She walked around the car and settled herself in the driver's seat, adjusting it and the rearview mirror slightly before clipping her seat belt and starting the car. She was pleased to see it was automatic. She could drive a stick shift well enough but in Auckland's rush-hour traffic, constantly riding the clutch would be a pain.

Wade's presence seemed to fill the car, not surprising given its compact size, but it was more than that. It was as if, by his very presence, he consumed her, too. Not just his presence, she realized, but his happiness. He was smiling and seemed genuinely content to drive around with her. She was struck by how much she'd missed this Wade—the Wade who enjoyed just being with her, as if he couldn't imagine anything better than an afternoon with her. Could she keep him like this—or would he revert back to his colder self at any moment?

"Everything okay?" he asked.

"Fine," she answered with a nervous smile.

She slid the car into gear, released the hand brake and drove the car down the driveway and out of the gates. The car handled beautifully. Certainly not in the same league as Wade's Porsche, or the snazzy little BMW her father had given her for her eighteenth birthday, but it certainly did the job. And it wouldn't make her stand out in the workplace car park, either.

When they returned home, Wade directed her to the new five-car garage at the rear of the house and indicated where her automatic door opener was. As they walked back to the house she thanked him again.

"No problem," he said. "I *was* being a jerk this morning. You manage to bring out the worst in me, Piper." They stopped under the porch by the kitchen door. "And I'm wondering, what are we going to do about it?"

Eight

"Just learn to be civil, I guess," she hedged in response.

But she knew exactly what he was talking about. They'd been circling each other like angry cats from the moment she'd arrived a few days ago. Antipathy was there, for sure, but beneath the surface lay something else. Something thick and heavy and powerful. Something neither of them wanted to acknowledge. It itched beneath their skin with a constant presence. An itch that she knew, without doubt, only one thing would assuage.

"Civil," he repeated. "You think that's the answer?"

She opened the kitchen door, letting out the warmth and golden light from within, dispelling the gloom outside.

"Maybe not, but it's the only one I can think of right now."

He took a step nearer, and rested a finger on her lips.

"Is that what you feel toward me now, Piper? Civility?"

Oh, God, no. She felt anything but. Given the opportunity, she'd open her mouth right now, draw his finger in and lave it with her tongue. She'd drive him crazy with wanting her and then eventually they'd do something about it, and maybe, just maybe, some of the tension between them would ease.

"Ah, so there the two of you are. What do you think of your new car?" Mrs. Dexter's voice broke the spell that bound them in the moment. "Come along inside and shut that door before you let all the warmth out. Dinner is almost ready."

Piper didn't know whether to be relieved at the interruption, or annoyed that she and Wade weren't going to pursue his question any further. In the end, she opted for relieved. It had been a demanding enough day so far already. She had no wish to complicate it further by exploring her feelings for him on a physical level right now.

Dinner was a mostly silent affair, punctuated only when she thought of questions to ask about Mitchell Exports that only Wade could answer. She wanted to return to the easy comfort she'd felt with him in the car, but ever since he'd stopped her outside the house, she'd been far too aware of him physically, tuned in to the tension rising between them.

Though the conversation was stilted, it was still instructive. She was beginning to feel a reluctant admiration for how he'd held everything together through her father's illness. Despite what he'd already told her, the other staff at the office today had informed her that Rex Mitchell had been forced to withdraw from business a whole lot earlier than she'd originally thought.

Not many of them made the connection that she was his daughter, thank goodness—and those who had, had also had the common courtesy not to bring it up in front of everyone else. She was lucky that Mitchell was a relatively common name. Most of her coworkers hadn't given it a second thought.

As Piper readied for bed that night, after setting out her clothes for the next day, she thought also of the university degree she'd never achieved. It would be both incredibly satisfying and useful to complete the papers she needed to finish her degree. What she'd learned before she left for overseas was a little rusty in the back of her mind. She could see how having the educational background would help her to grasp the running of Mitchell Exports a whole lot faster.

Wade might not realize it yet, but she planned on being an integral part of the company. It was something she'd always wanted to do at her father's side from when she'd been a little girl and finally understood what it was that kept him from home, from her, for so many hours a day. She'd wanted to be a part of it, a part of *his* world, a part of him. But Rex had never believed she was competent to do more than spend his money. Beating her head against his chauvinism for so many years had eventually done her in and driven her to behave stupidly. Now, inasmuch as she was capable, she was bound and determined to prove to Wade she could be something, someone, worthy of working there.

As she slipped between the fine cotton lavender-scented sheets, she resolved to find out what she could do about furthering her studies. She fell asleep happy in the knowledge that she was finally on the right track with her life. And if she could make this thing, the constant simmering heat between her and Wade, into something real and lasting along the way, to build a real future for herself and Wade and their baby, then all the better.

The days began to blur into routine. She'd wake and dress for work, always leaving the house after Wade, and usually getting home before him. She knew he was keeping an eye on her in the office but so far, aside from one invoicing incident, so good. Thankfully, Jane had picked up on the mistake before it had gone any further but Piper imagined that it otherwise would have resulted in a warning, and she didn't want to give Wade any reason to end her employment.

The prospect of earning her own wage was exhilarating. It was the first time in her life that she'd been gainfully employed. While she'd worked herself to exhaustion with her volunteer stints, and had gained a deep satisfaction in her achievements, this was quite different.

It was Friday afternoon, at the end of her first week of work, when she was asked to join a group of the staff at a nearby pub for a quiet weekend wind-down drink. Wade had been out of the office all day with clients. No doubt he'd be wining and dining late into the night and since it was also the Dexters' night off, Piper didn't relish going home to an empty house. But when she joined her new colleagues, she also didn't feel as if she fit in. They were full of gossip about boyfriends and mutual acquaintances. It left her feeling on the periphery of what her life should have been all this time. In the end she made her apologies after only half a glass of wine, and shot away home.

There were a few lights on in the house, she noticed as she rolled along the driveway. Wade's bedroom lights were among them. She parked her car in the garage and walked along the covered walkway that led to the back entrance of the house. More lights were on in the kitchen. Maybe the Dexters hadn't gone out after all. But the instant she set foot inside she knew they weren't home.

There was a very strong male presence in the room, a very singular strong male presence. Wade stood at the stove top, dressed casually but all in black, and with a plain white apron slung around his hips. A rich aroma redolent with tomato, garlic and a hint of spice filled the air. Instantly her mouth watered.

"What's this?" Piper asked, deliberately pitching her voice to be light and airy as if his mere presence wasn't enough to send her pulse racing. "Your take on *MasterChef?*"

He looked up from the pot he was stirring and flung her a smile. "No, I wish. In fact you might wish so, too, when you taste it. I like to cook but rarely have the time."

"I imagine Dexie doesn't let you over her threshold much,

anyway, at least not to do anything but eat," Piper commented dryly.

Mrs. Dexter's proprietary manner over her domain was legendary. Wade chuckled in response to her comment.

"No, you're right. I only get to play on her nights off. Why don't you go upstairs and get changed. I'll have dinner ready in about half an hour or so. Here, take this up with you."

He reached for an open bottle of wine on the kitchen table and poured her a glass of red. She sniffed the bouquet appreciatively before taking a sip.

"Mmm, that's lovely. Is it a new label? I don't think I've seen that one before."

"You won't have. It's from a new winery down in the south island near Wanaka. I've been in meetings with the owner and winemaker most of today. We'll be handling their exports into the South Pacific."

"Well, I sure hope they'll be keeping some stock for domestic sale." She took another sip. "You said half an hour. Any chance we can stretch that out a bit?"

He shrugged. "I suppose so, why?"

"I just thought I'd like to take a bath before dinner, help me get the kinks out after sitting at a desk all day."

"Regretting it, Piper?" he asked, his face inscrutable as he watched for her response.

"No, of course not. I'm just not used to being in one place doing one thing all day long."

"Go on, take your time," he said, taking a sip of his own wine. "Everything will keep."

She ducked her head in acknowledgment and left the room, full of surprising anticipation. This felt like a date. And she had to admit, she liked it.

Wade watched her go, and wondered if she'd have been so relaxed if she'd known exactly what he had in store for her tonight. He turned the heat down on the pots on the stove and settled at the kitchen table absently swirling his wine in his glass as he played with the paper—the medical report—he'd left on the table.

They were all systems go. The news had left him with mixed feelings. Gaining some sort of dominance over Piper, making her regret her actions when she'd left New Zealand, how she'd treated both him and Rex—those had all been driving motivations for him. But she'd surprised him since her return. Sure, she was still as feisty as ever, but it had a purpose now. While she hadn't been above making her demands about him creating a job for her at Mitchell Exports, she had impressed him with her fight for independence over getting to work and starting from the ground up. Not to mention her aptitude in the workplace.

Maybe Rex had been wrong about her. He'd often wondered why the older man had been so adamant that she be wrapped in cotton wool and never be allowed to experience the ugliness of the big wide world they lived in. He could understand the urge to protect her, to smooth away hardship from her path, but had Piper felt dismissed by her father's unwillingness to let her into the business side of his life?

Wade thought back to the first time he'd met her on a day when she'd come to the office to coerce her father out to lunch. Rex had refused, suggesting instead that she take Wade. He'd seen the flash of hurt in her eyes. Hurt rapidly followed by an equally swift flash of anger.

That lunch had been interesting. Piper had been equal parts amusing, tempting and terrifying. And underneath it all he'd sensed a vulnerability in her, almost a need for approval. He'd laughed often at her clever conversation and couldn't fail to notice how she'd bloomed at the attention he gave her. Looking back, it was as if she hadn't trusted that her intelligence would be enough to snare him, so she'd had to use her physical wiles to ensure she had him where they both wanted to be. How had he never noticed that before? Of course, he'd been younger then, and he'd have been blind and stupid not to have been attracted to her on a physical level, or to have ignored her blatant flirtation. A flirtation that had rapidly led to other things. "Things" that he hoped to resume tonight.

He still wanted a child, wanted all he'd demanded when he'd laid out their agreement. But he was finally allowing himself to admit how much he'd missed having her in his bed.

Piper soon returned downstairs. She topped up his glass and refilled hers before taking a seat at the table.

"Is there anything I can do to help? Set the table, maybe?" she asked.

"No, everything's all ready. You can take our glasses through to the dining room, though. I'll bring the tray with our meal."

"We're eating in the dining room?"

"Sure, why not? Why? Don't you think my cooking will be worth it?"

May as well aim for offhand, he thought, because the evening was going to get serious before very long.

She flicked him a glance but grabbed their glasses and the bottle and did as he suggested. He quickly took a pair of covered dishes from the oven where they'd been warming and placed them and a bowl filled with freshly tossed salad onto the large butler's tray and followed her.

He heard her gasp as she entered the room, and smiled a secret smile. The scene was set, and he wanted her to enjoy it. Wanted to make this night so much more than just fulfilling an agreement.

"This looks amazing," Piper commented as he laid the tray on its stand and transferred the dishes onto protective mats on the mahogany table.

Wade cast a glance at the highly polished silverware, the

ornately embellished candelabra gleaming under the glow of tall crimson candles and the sparkling crystal.

"Thanks," he answered simply as he crossed to where he'd laid her place setting and pulled out her chair.

"You've gone to a lot of bother," Piper said.

"I think the end of your first week at work calls for a celebration, don't you?" he asked as he settled into his chair at the head of the table.

"Yes." She nodded, as if surprised to be reminded. "It does. Thank you."

Wade gestured to the hot dishes in the center of the table. "Would you like me to serve or would you prefer to help yourself?"

"Oh, let me do something. I'll dish it up for us."

She leaned forward, the action exposing the curve of one breast inside the deep V-necked top she wore. The color, a deep blush pink, suited her but he thought the color better matched the tip of the one pink nipple he'd glimpsed as she'd moved. Instantly he was rock hard for her. His mouth dry and his skin stretched taut across his body. He wanted to dispense with the formalities. To forgo the niceties of dining together, of slowing wooing her, but he'd promised himself he'd take it slow.

"Wade?"

Piper's voice dragged him back into the present. She gestured to his plate. She'd served him and he hadn't even noticed, he'd been so wrapped up in his reaction to her.

"Thanks," he said, although his voice sounded strained even to his ears. He reached for his glass and lifted it in her direction. "Let's make a toast. To your first week at Mitchell Exports."

"And to many more," she amended as she clinked her glass with his. She sipped her wine before putting down her glass and lifting her fork. "This is beef stroganoff, right? Did you make it from scratch? It smells divine."

Wade pretended to be mortally wounded that she would think he'd resorted to a packet. "Of course, I made it with my own fair hands," he insisted. "What do you think?"

He watched as she lifted the fork to her mouth and tasted the rich mixture of beef and sauce. She chewed slowly before closing her eyes on a moan of pure pleasure. He swallowed. This evening wasn't going to get anymore comfortable any time soon. He'd better hunker down to weather it out.

"This is fantastic. And you really made it from scratch?" She gave another appreciative moan. "No wonder Dexie keeps you out of the kitchen. You're fierce competition."

He felt his cheeks heat a little under the compliment. "She's got no fear of me treading on her toes. I have a few dishes I do well, that I enjoy preparing, but for the rest I'm quite happy to be fed by someone else."

"Well, at least you'd never starve if you were on your own. I'm hopeless in the kitchen."

"Maybe you just need someone to take the time to teach you," he remarked.

For a minute she looked pensive. "I often wonder what my life would have been like if my mother had lived. Whether I'd have had the chance to learn things like cooking, keeping house properly. Dexie is so capable at everything but she doesn't tolerate fools. She's always been inclined to shoo me away when I've wanted to help her."

Piper had been so much younger than him when she'd lost her mother. At least he'd still had memories to cling to when the going got tough. It couldn't have been easy for her—a distant father and older family retainers meant no loving arms to welcome her each and every day.

"Do you remember your mother?"

"Not really, just hints of things. Like the smell of her perfume or the sound of her laughter. Sometimes I wonder whether they're real or if they're just related to other things and people from when I was growing up. I know Dad loved her dearly. Sometimes I wonder if he didn't die inside when he lost her."

"It certainly can't be easy losing a partner."

"You lost your mother, too. Do you remember her well?"

"Sure, and I count myself lucky for that if nothing else. Life was different when she was around. She made every day fun."

His voice trailed into silence. The fun had irrevocably ceased when his mother had passed away suddenly from an undiagnosed heart condition. Life after that had become very dark indeed, especially when the Family Court and Children's Services had become involved. He shook his head.

"Listen to us, we're supposed to be celebrating, not getting all maudlin."

Piper smiled back at him, but he noticed her smile didn't quite reach her eyes. Wade devoted himself to ensuring the rest of the meal continued in a far lighter vein. It was important to him to chase the shadows away for her, for reasons that no longer involved his agenda for their evening.

Nine

They'd cleared the table and put the plates in the dishwasher. Piper was amazed at how comfortable and domestic it all felt with just the two of them, alone. Wade had been fabulous company throughout the evening, showing a side of himself that she'd missed from their earlier months together—the months before she'd ruined everything by setting herself in total competition against her father for Wade's attention. She'd loved Wade with a passion that had frightened her at times with its intensity and she hadn't known how to handle it, or him. And to her shame, she'd resented anyone else who'd had a place in his heart.

She'd been so immature. She could have had them both, instead she'd ended up with neither. And now, she had Wade in a legal contract that had nothing to do with emotion or love.

Sometimes she wished she could simply turn back the clock and make better choices. But then she'd temper that with what she'd learned along her journey. It was a rite of passage she'd had to, *needed* to, go through on her own to really learn what was important in life.

"Do you feel like a nightcap?" Wade asked as he straightened from loading the last of the plates in the dishwasher.

"What were you thinking?" she asked.

"How about a twenty-year-old tawny port?"

"Sounds lovely. In the library?"

"No, I was thinking about in my sitting room."

Piper raised her eyebrows. "Your sitting room? I didn't know you had one."

"When the property was signed over to me I did some remodeling of the guest suite upstairs."

The guest suite. That had originally been her parents' suite until her mother's death, at which time her father had relocated farther down the hall.

"I'd like to see what you've done," she said, even as anticipation mingled with unease curled in the pit of her stomach.

It was one thing having an intimate dinner together in neutral territory, but being in an area that was solely Wade's domain, that really was something else.

"Come on, then," Wade said, holding the kitchen door open for her and gesturing for her to precede him.

They ascended the stairs together and as they walked the length of the landing that led to his suite, Piper felt her apprehension develop even further.

"Have a seat and make yourself comfortable," he said as he opened the door for her.

Piper was taken aback the moment she stepped foot inside the door. The room wasn't as she'd expected. Somehow she'd imagined he'd have gone for dark, heavy furnishings, similar to what her father had done in his rooms. Yet there was a comfort and lightness about the room that made it instantly welcoming. Welcoming, and yet there was also something else. An ambience that suggested a very particular kind of welcome. She sat down on one of the comfortable caramel-colored leather sofas arranged in front of the fireplace.

Even the air in the room suggested an atmosphere of sensuous luxury and well-being. Wade stepped forward and lit a series of candles that decorated the wide mantelpiece over the fireplace. Behind the antique fire screen, embers glowed warm and inviting in the grate. He added another log to the fire, sending a shower of sparks flying up the chimney.

"I had the fireplace redone and the chimney cleared when I took over these rooms. It seemed a great pity not to make the most of it, especially on cooler nights like this," he said, dusting his hands lightly.

Piper moved to the end of the sofa, closer to the fireplace, and put out her hands to the warmth from the flames that were already licking the log. To her surprise her hands were trembling. She clenched them into fists and thrust them back into her lap. She was just here for a nightcap, so why was she so nervous? Behind her she heard the clink of crystal against crystal as Wade poured a measure of port into each of the glasses he'd had prepared on a tray.

She hadn't missed seeing them there as they'd entered the room, as if he'd known all along he'd be sharing a drink with her, here, tonight. She turned to face him, accepting the drink he'd poured her and fighting to ignore the quiver of awareness that sparked up her arm at the casual touch of his fingers against hers.

"Wade? Is there something else behind tonight? Something you're not telling me?"

"What makes you ask?" he answered, his gaze meeting hers unwaveringly.

"It's just…oh, I don't know. I just feel as if you have some kind of agenda going on here."

"Agenda," he repeated, as if testing the word on his tongue. "I suppose you could say that," he admitted.

She froze as he shoved one hand deep into his trouser

pocket and pulled out a crumpled sheet of paper. He handed it to her. Piper put her drink on a side table and took the paper, smoothing it out on the arm of the chair. Her eyes blurred a little as she attempted to read the words printed upon the sheet. She blinked and tried again. This time they made total sense.

She lifted her face to look at Wade who had seated himself opposite her on the matching sofa, his legs outstretched, his feet crossed at his ankles. He looked as relaxed and as comfortable as a man could get but she could see the lines of tension around his mouth and eyes. He was waiting for her to respond.

"So we're all systems go, then," she said, her voice cracking on the words and making a total lie of her insouciant shot at delivery.

"Yes, we are."

She waited for him to say something more but instead he just sat there, watching her. She felt her skin prickle under his regard, but it wasn't an uncomfortable sensation. More stimulating than unpleasant. She shifted on the sofa, trying to ease the tension building inside her. She should have known it would be futile. The movement made her thighs brush together, causing her inner muscles to involuntarily clench.

She swallowed and reached for her glass of port, taking a sip before putting the glass down again.

"And when do you suggest we begin to...?"

She couldn't bring herself to say the words. Not out loud. Wade, it transpired, had no such compunction.

"Make our baby?" he asked. "No harm in starting right now."

She froze in her chair. "N-now?"

"What's the matter, Piper? Do you have any objections?"

He rose from his seat then settled his body down on the sofa next to hers. Instant heat emanated along her side. Heat that spread across her shoulders as he draped one arm casually across the back of the sofa, behind her.

"No," she denied, even though everything inside her screamed yes.

"Then you won't mind me doing this," Wade said softly.

He lifted one hand and turned her face toward him, then moved forward to seal her lips with his in a smooth movement that spoke volumes as to his determination. His lips were gentle against hers, teasing, coaxing. Not the ravishment she'd expected. Inch by inch she felt her body relax. The man certainly knew how to kiss.

His fingers traced lightly along her jawline, before sliding behind her ear to cup her head.

"I've wanted to do this for days," he groaned against her mouth.

She was lost for a reply. Part of her was insanely glad he'd been suffering the same desires as she had—with the emphasis on suffering. But the other part of her was in a state of chaos. She had known all along this day, or night, would come. But now it was here, she knew she was most definitely not ready. Oh, yes, on a physical level there was no question she was up for this. In fact it would be a relief to actually get down and dirty with him. But on an emotional level? She didn't know if she could come out of this without some serious harm.

Wade's lips began a new onslaught, this time down the fine cord of her neck. Oh, she thought—as fire raced through her, sending all her senses aflame and clouding the thoughts that tossed around in her mind—he remembered. Her neck had always been a major erogenous zone for her. Especially that part just behind—

"Oh!" she gasped as his lips found the tender skin behind her ear.

"You still like that?" he growled softly.

In response she let her head fall to the other side, exposing her sensitive spot and giving him unobstructed access. He didn't let her down. He used his tongue and his lips in an alternating assault, while his hand lifted the edge of her top and his fingers traced a steady path to her breasts. She squirmed as he allowed his hand to linger on its journey, her body all but screaming out for his touch in other tender places.

"Let's get rid of this, shall we?" he said, now gripping the bottom of her top with both hands and beginning to pull it off for her.

She assisted as much as she was able, her breath catching in her throat as he paused and allowed his eyes to feast upon her naked breasts. The stark appreciation evident there sent a flood of heat to her core.

"And you," she said, her voice shaking. "Let's get rid of yours as well, hmm?"

He helped her pull off the black sweater that had clung to his muscled shoulders and coasted over his upper torso. And what a torso. If a man could ever be described as beautiful, Wade was very definitely that man. While not bulked up with muscle, there was no denying the latent strength beneath his pale golden skin. A light smattering of hair sprinkled from the middle of his chest, before thinning out into a line that arrowed down to the waistband of his trousers.

She reached for his belt buckle and murmured a tiny sound of protest when he grabbed her hands in his. But the protest turned to a deep-throated sound of satisfaction when he pulled her to her feet and continued to undress her. Skimming the elastic-waisted yoga pants she'd worn down her legs, then removing the tiny scrap of sheer satin and lace panties with equal grace.

He even moved beautifully, she registered as she watched him undo his belt buckle and zipper and remove his pants and briefs in one smooth motion. Next came his socks and then he was standing there before her, male perfection in all its glory. Wade bent and gathered the soft cushions off the sofas and cast them on the floor in front of the fireplace before guiding her down onto them.

She expected him to join her but he crossed the room and flicked a switch, turning off all the lights so that she was bathed only in the illumination of the fire and the golden glow cast by the candles above it. She stretched against the pillows and smiled as he walked back toward her.

Without saying a single word, he lay down beside her and began to touch, at first featherlight caresses designed to titillate and tease. And tease they did. She felt her nipples tighten into hard buds, felt moisture gather at the apex of her thighs. Felt her need for him, for his total possession, increase in steady increments until she was mindless for anything else.

And then he changed his tactics. He shifted his body over hers, stretching up her arms above her head and securing her wrists with one hand while supporting his weight with the other. The torture began with his tongue and his mouth, with the hot, heavy weight of his arousal against her body.

"Let me touch you," she whispered. "I want to touch you."

"Not yet. A man can only exert so much control, Piper, and I want this to be good for us both."

The knowledge that he was holding on by a fine thread only ignited her more. She squirmed against him, feeling his erection at her entrance and wondering just how hard she'd have to push to drive him over the edge of control and into abandon. She didn't have to wonder for long. His entire body shuddered as she moved sinuously against him.

"You're not making it easy for me," he said.

"I don't want it to be easy for you." She smiled up at him. "I want you to feel everything just as much as I am."

"Oh, believe me, I do."

He caught her mouth with his and gave her a deep wet kiss that left her in no doubt as to how close he was to capitulating. She gave back as good as she got, taking his tongue into her mouth and suckling it, using every trick she could to get him to give in. And then, oh, glory, he let go of her hands.

Immediately she reached out to touch him, to stroke his shoulders, his chest, to pull lightly at his nipples. He retaliated in kind, with his teeth and his tongue against her own, drawing her nipples, one then the other, into his mouth and releasing them, over and over. She drifted her hands lower, past his waist, to his hips and then, to his groin. His penis was hard and hot, a drop of moisture already pooling at its tip. She stroked him, holding him firmly in the grip of her fist, and felt him shudder against her again.

Piper let her legs fall open and guided him to her entrance, rubbing his blunt head against her moisture. His hand covered hers, positioning himself just inside her. His entire body shook as he waited there, his eyes, glittering chips of granite, meshed with hers. She lifted her hips and felt him slide a little farther within her. A tiny cry spilled from her lips. She surged against him again, wanting to take him deeper still—yet his hand over hers prevented it. How could he just stay there? She was desperate now. Desperate for his full possession.

"Wade, please?" she begged, her hips still riding him as much as he allowed.

"Yes," he answered, the single syllable a raw sound on the air between them.

He took his hand away and she grabbed at his hips with both of hers, angling her pelvis and waiting for his full possession. When it came, it drove the air from her lungs and thought from her mind as her body clenched around him. His length surged within her, again and again, driving her to higher peaks with each thrust. She couldn't keep her eyes open any longer, sensation took over her body, starbursts of light danced behind her eyelids. Wave after wave of pleasure built inside her. Wave after wave that grew until her entire body exploded from sheer intensity. Expanding ripples of ecstasy undulated through her, finally easing in force until her body fell back against the cushions filled with a delicious lassitude that invaded every cell in her body.

Wade collapsed against her, his back slick with perspiration, his buttocks and thighs still clenched beneath her touch. She could feel him pulsing rhythmically within her, feel the heat of his climax against her womb.

She'd never before felt this level of synchronicity, of bliss—not even with Wade eight years ago. What had just happened between them fell on the scale of cataclysmic. Even through her pleasure-hazed stupor, she was aware of her heart beating erratically in her chest and her pulse skipping through her veins with the speed of a madly galloping stallion. And he was no different. His breathing was ragged, and she could feel his body throb with the velocity of his own pulse.

"I didn't hurt you, did I?" he asked, his voice muffled against her neck.

Piper laughed softly. "Hurt me? You have to be kidding."

He went to lift himself off her but she wrapped her legs around his and her arms about his waist and held him close, keeping him trapped inside her at the same time.

"I'm too heavy for you," he protested.

"No, you're not. Stay, I don't want to lose this feeling just yet."

Wade sighed in response, his breath warm and moist against her sensitized skin. Her inner muscles tensed, pulling against him one more time as an aftershock of pleasure fluttered to her very core.

She hadn't felt this good, this satisfied, in her living memory. She wasn't about to do a single thing to change that right now. Her eyes slid shut and she continued to hold Wade to her, reveling in his heaviness and warmth, and hoping against hope that they'd conceived their baby with all their barriers down—with nothing between them but perhaps the hope that things might just work out after all.

* * *

Piper woke much later to the sound of rain once more hammering against the windows. The candles on the mantelpiece had long since gutted in their containers, the last of the embers in the fireplace now casting the only light in the room.

Wade's weight kept her pinned to the cushions and rug beneath her. Not the most comfortable position she'd ever slept in, she thought, but far from the worst, either. She trailed a hand down his back. Oh, how she loved the feel of his skin, especially where it touched hers. He was strength and hardness combined with an intrinsic thread of gentleness woven through at the same time. A man of contrasts.

He'd make a great father.

The thought shocked her. She'd never thought of Wade in terms of being a dad. She'd heard him talk about it, allowed herself to be locked into this agreement between them. Allowed? She wrinkled her forehead as she considered the concept, and forced herself to acknowledge that which she'd been trying to avoid all along. She could have just said no to him. Left him to see what the worst was that he could have done to her. She had no money. She had no home. No court in the land could have made her pay what she didn't have.

So why had she allowed him to bully her into signing?

Could it be that she still loved him? As the thought blossomed, she forced herself to acknowledge the real truth. The truth that resounded through her mind with a single word.

Yes.

Ten

She must have made a sound or a movement that disturbed Wade.

"Are you okay? I didn't mean to fall asleep on you like that."

"It's all right," she answered, still reeling from the certainty she'd only just acknowledged.

Wade shifted his weight off her and traced the bone structure of her face with one hand as he lay on his side next to her.

"I'd better get to my bed," Piper said, moving away from him.

"Why?" he asked.

"Well, we've...you know." She waved her hand futilely.

He laughed. She seemed to have that effect on him a lot lately.

"What's so funny?" she said, prickling at his response.

"That you think I'm going to let you go."

He got to his feet in a single movement and reached out a

hand to help her up. Keeping her hand captive within his, he guided her to a door that led off the sitting room. He swung it open and drew her toward a massive four-poster bed. Swags of heavy fabric, pointed with gold tassels, hung from the four points.

"Very Lord of the Manor," Piper commented as Wade pulled back the covers and ushered her within the sheets.

"Very." He smiled in return and followed her into the bed.

The contrast of his warm body and the cool sheets against her skin sent a tingle through her nerves. A tingle that intensified as Wade's arm curled around her and one hand began to play with the short thatch of hair at her groin, every now and then slipping a little lower to graze against the taut bud hidden there.

"Hey, that's not fair," she said when she could catch a breath.

"Indulge me," came the command from behind her.

His erection slid between her legs and she hitched herself up a little letting him enter her fully.

"Since you're so persuasive, I think I will."

His penetration hit just the right spot and she could feel the rising pleasure begin to radiate with every drive of his hips. She moved with him, wanting more with every stroke. His fingers didn't let up their offensive either and it was only a few minutes before she began to feel her body coil tightly as her orgasm built and built.

"Too much," she cried into the pillow.

"Never too much," he replied, his hips now picking up the pace and driving her over the edge until her body spasmed in paroxysms of satisfaction.

Wade held on as long as he could, but his body had other ideas. The force and strength of Piper's orgasm was his complete undoing and he gave over to the gratification his body demanded.

He continued to hold Piper long after she'd fallen back into an exhausted sleep, his fingers tracing tiny circles on the smooth, soft skin of her belly. Who knew? Maybe they'd already started a new life tonight. The mere thought was enough to make something in his chest clench in anticipation.

One thing was certain, though, he would do everything to ensure this baby made it. He would be there through every single step of this pregnancy and thereafter. A virtual slide show ran through his head of his child's life, with him there for him or her at every pass.

He chose to ignore the quirk of his mind that placed a smiling image of Piper right at his side.

Wade woke late that morning, surprised to find his arms and his bed bereft of Piper's warmth. He flicked a glance at his bedside clock and was amazed to see it was already nine o'clock. He couldn't remember the last time he'd slept that late, not even with an unhealthy dose of jet lag.

He hurried through his shower and getting dressed and went downstairs. Piper was seated at the kitchen table, the remnants of her breakfast on the plate pushed to one side, her attention focused on the bundles of paper scattered on the surface in front of her.

"Good morning," he said as he came in.

"Morning," she replied, not even lifting her head from her perusal of what looked like a prospectus of some kind. "I put your breakfast in the oven to keep warm."

"Ah yes, the Dexters are away this whole weekend, aren't they?"

Piper nodded. Obviously not up for a huge amount of morning-after conversation, he observed wryly as he lifted his plate from the oven.

"Hot!" he yelped as he rapidly transferred the plate from his hand to the placemat opposite where Piper sat.

"I did say I'd put your breakfast in the oven to keep warm," she said, finally looking up to meet his eyes.

"So you did." He lifted the foil off the top of his plate and grinned appreciatively. "I see you haven't lost your touch with a good old-fashioned breakfast."

"I was hungry this morning," she admitted, a flush of color lighting her cheeks.

"So am I," he answered, but kept his gaze very firmly upon her.

To his delight her blush deepened and spread and she quickly averted her eyes, transferring her attention back to the booklet in her hand.

"What's that you have there?" he asked as he poured himself a cup of coffee before sitting down opposite her.

"Nothing much," she hedged.

He reached across the table and with one finger pushed the booklet up in her hands until he could see the front cover clearly. A university prospectus?

"Looks like a bit more than *nothing much* to me. Are you thinking about going back to Uni?" Wade fought to hide his surprise.

She nodded. "Do you have a problem with that?"

"Not if it doesn't interfere with your current commitments."

"My work at Mitchell Exports? I don't think you need to worry about that. It's hardly taxing what I'm doing there."

"True, but I was talking about your commitment to me." More particularly, her commitment to their possibly already conceived child. He didn't want her to overtire herself or to put herself or their baby at risk.

She gave him a hard look and pushed her chair back from the table. "Trust me, you won't have anything to worry about."

Wouldn't he? He certainly hoped she was right. He didn't want to stand in the way of her bettering herself, if that was what she really wanted. "Perhaps you should let me be the judge of what I worry about." He forced a smile.

"What are you looking at enrolling for?"

"I thought I'd find out how I can supplement what I did

before I went overseas. I would like to finish my business degree, if possible."

Finish her degree? "But you only completed a couple papers before and that was eight years ago. What makes you think you can just pick up where you left off?"

"I don't know if I can, that's why I'm looking into the courses and pre-enrollment information now."

"Piper, you were hardly an A-grade student. This is really going to take time and perseverance. Don't you think you're biting off more than you can chew?"

"Well, thanks. It's nice to know where you stand. I would have thought you'd be happy to see me doing something so that I can eventually support myself."

"Is that what this is about? I already told you that, as long as you're under my roof, I will cover your expenses."

"Good, then you can pay for my tuition."

Piper rose from her chair and gathered her papers.

"That wasn't what I meant," Wade said firmly.

"Fine, so I'll apply for a student loan."

Before he could reply she'd left the kitchen with her nose very firmly in the air. Wade watched her go with narrowed eyes. Piper? Back at Uni? She looked, and sounded, as if she was serious about this. If she was, then of course he'd make sure she had the financial support she needed to make it happen. But he still struggled to reconcile the girl he'd once thought he knew so well with the determined young woman of today.

Piper fought back the tears that smarted in her eyes. She felt so stupid. She'd have thought that maybe Wade would understand why it would be a good thing for her to complete her degree but he was no different from her father. It seemed they were cut from the same cloth after all. Both determined to pigeonhole her. And no matter what she did to try and prove her worth—to garner their love and respect for her as a person—they wouldn't see it. No wonder the two men had gotten on so well. Perhaps leaving them both had been the best decision she'd ever made. Certainly better than the one she'd made to come home.

It had been nothing but heartache, and challenge after challenge since her return. Drawing water by hand from a well or clearing away a mudslide so a medical team could pass a road suddenly looked like easier options.

She let herself into the morning room, the room that had been her mother's, and threw herself onto the chaise. Why did everything have to be so hard?

In a perfect world she'd be able to declare her feelings for Wade, and of course he'd reciprocate and they'd both live happily ever after. A cynical laugh bubbled in her chest. As if. No, there was one thing and one thing only that Wade wanted from her and it was definitely not her lifelong devotion.

She rubbed one hand absently over her lower stomach. She'd felt him do the same last night. Had he been wondering, as she did now, whether they'd conceived the child he so desperately wanted?

A sound at the door drove her to her feet. Wade came inside the morning room and stopped just one step from the door.

"Are you absolutely serious about finishing your degree?" he asked, an inscrutable expression on his face.

"Of course I am, why else would I have gone to the bother of getting all this?" She waved the clutch of papers she held in her hand at him. "I need this, Wade. I need it for me. I know I bummed around the last time. I was in a different head space then. I didn't appreciate any of what I had, I just knew I wanted it all." She shot him a glance that she hoped reiterated that he had been among those things she'd wanted so very much. "When I couldn't have what I wanted, I behaved like an idiot. I know that. I just think I deserve a second chance. I really want to get it right this time."

She'd said more than she'd wanted to, far, far more than

she'd wanted to. Right now she wouldn't blame him if he out-right laughed in her face and walked away but to her surprise he held out his hand.

"May I see the courses you're looking at taking?"

Silently she handed over the information and watched as he settled into a chair and flicked through it all. Finally he looked up again.

"You *really* want to do this?"

"I really do."

He leaned back in his chair and looked up at her. Despite her having the physical advantage, it certainly didn't feel that way. For a long moment he said nothing and the silence stretched out painfully between them. He cleared his throat before speaking. "If you're absolutely serious about this—"

"Oh, yes. I am," she interrupted.

"If you'll let me finish," he said with a small but genuine smile.

"Sure, go on. I'm sorry."

"As I was saying, if you're absolutely serious about this then you may be eligible to do these papers through Mitchell Exports. We run cadetships, much like your father used to do unpaid internships, but this way you get to earn as you learn. We have strict entry criteria and a panel made up of management personnel at Mitchell Exports has the final decision. Are you prepared to be scrutinized and assessed to see if you're deemed worthy?"

Scrutinized? Assessed? It sounded daunting. The old Piper would have laughed in his face then run a mile in the opposite direction. But she'd had to change and she really needed to prove to herself that she could do this.

"Yes," she answered simply. "I'll do whatever it takes."

"It's not going to be a walk in the park, Piper. You will have to apply yourself at work and here at home in the evenings. The study load is huge. Are you sure you will be able to cope with that?"

"Don't underestimate how much this means to me, Wade. I am determined to do this."

"And when you fall pregnant?"

"I don't see why I can't continue to study. I remember pregnant women and young mothers at Uni when I was there. I'll find a balance. Look, I don't expect to achieve this overnight. I'm being realistic. I know it won't be easy for me to get back into a learning mind-set, let alone a lecture environment. But I will do it."

Her earnestness must have convinced him.

"I'll discuss it with the team on Monday and we'll go from there, okay?"

"Thank you," she said.

It was far more than she'd expected of him. Far more than she deserved given her track record.

"Just don't let me down on this."

"I won't."

As autumn slid wetly into winter, Wade found himself having to reassess his opinion of Piper on a regular basis, both in the office and at home. Her application to her work had seen her become immensely popular with the staff and her intervention when she'd seen a mistake in a proposal written in Spanish, targeting a sought-after South American client, had saved them both embarrassment and thousands of dollars.

When had she learned Spanish? he wondered as he signed off on the new deal with a flourish of his pen. And what else had she learned in the years they'd been apart?

By day she was a diligent employee. Outside of business hours, she was an equally diligent student as she worked through a six-month-long pre-entry course to get up to speed for attending university again for the semester beginning in the new year. And by night—he felt that all too familiar tightening in his groin—by night she was an exceptional lover.

He looked forward to their evenings together with an enthusiasm he'd underestimated. Sex with Piper had always been good, but what they shared now surpassed anything they'd experienced before. There was a synchronicity in their movements, their desire to give one another pleasure and receive it in return. Aside from when she'd had her period some weeks ago, they'd spent every night making love. Even then he hadn't allowed her to return to her room and had instead enjoyed the closeness of simply holding her in his arms at night.

This new Piper was indeed someone else compared to the woman who'd left after demanding he give up his life's dream to follow her overseas on a tantrum-induced-whim. It was as if she was doing her level best to please and it occurred to him that above all else, Piper craved acceptance. Everything she did was with the purpose of fitting in with her peers, and of gaining a degree of respect and independence.

Last week he'd reviewed the accounts that related to the running of the house and cars and noted that there was no bill for the petrol she'd been putting in her car. On checking up with the gas station, he'd been informed that Piper was paying for her fills herself and not charging them to the account he'd had set up. When he'd approached her, she'd merely lifted her chin in that endearingly self-reliant way of hers, and said she was earning a decent wage so there was no reason why she couldn't meet her own costs. He'd wanted to argue with her, to tell her that providing for her was his responsibility now, but there had been something in her stance that made him think twice about pushing the point home.

Deep down he recognized and understood her need to stand on her own two feet—it was how he'd felt his entire life—and for some reason that commonality with her was as unsettling as it was encouraging.

He wondered anew why Rex had never encouraged Piper to achieve more with her life. Why had the man kept his daughter slotted within set confines of behavior and expectation? No wonder Piper previously had never amounted to anything more than a two-dimensional woman whose selfish demands had clouded what Wade now believed were the real issues that drove her.

She was an intelligent woman who had a quick grasp of business concepts. Not only that, but her keen mind presented solutions to issues that he would have expected from someone with a great deal of life experience. Just what *had* she done while she was away? What had made her come into her potential that he'd only ever glimpsed in the past?

Rex had done her a disservice. If the old man had perhaps been a little less chauvinistic and a whole lot more inclined to see beyond the peripheral beauty of his daughter, he could have had a formidable business partner at his side when he got sick. He could have kept Mitchell Exports a family owned business, instead of sharing that honor with the son of a stranger.

This softening in attitude to Piper was a new concept for Wade. For so many years he'd been focused on his anger toward her, on his need to even what he saw as a score to be settled between them. Now, he could at least accept that her behavior had not all been her own fault.

He shook his head slightly. Man, he must be getting soft. He'd never have believed he could feel like this about Piper again—protective, encouraging.

Wade put down his pen and picked up the contracts before rising from his desk and going to his PA.

"Could you see these are couriered to Mr. Rodriguez as quickly as possible?" he asked, leaving the contracts on the side of her desk.

"Sure thing," his PA replied. "Oh, and Piper called and left a message for you. She wasn't feeling quite a hundred percent so she headed home early today."

"She's not feeling well?" Wade asked. "Do you know why?"

"Not sure, could be the flu. She started here after we all had our annual flu shots."

Flu, or could it be something else that made her feel sick? Whatever it was he needed to find out face-to-face.

"Cancel the rest of my appointments," he instructed as he headed for the door.

"But—"

His PA's protest fell on deaf ears as the door swung closed behind him. Anything and everything else faded into insignificance. He had to know and he had to know right now.

Was Piper pregnant?

Eleven

Traffic on the way home was heavy, despite the early hour. Schools hadn't closed yet for the day, yet there seemed to be an inordinate number of cars on the road. And the rain didn't help at all. Coming down across the windshield in driving sheets, Wade's wipers were working flat out to keep the glass clear.

Everything crawled to a standstill near the turn off to his street. Up ahead, though, Wade caught a glimpse of red and blue flashing lights. Police, a fire truck and an ambulance? A sick feeling of dread took up residence in his gut. Without sparing the weather another thought, Wade pulled his car over to the side and got out, running toward the cause of the traffic jam. As he neared the intersection, the dread solidified into abject terror. There, wrapped around a power pole, was an all-too-familiar vehicle. Piper's car!

Rain streaming down his face and in his eyes, Wade elbowed past the gathering crowd. Nothing else mattered right now but knowing that she was okay.

A team of firefighters were using cutting equipment to free the driver's door of her car.

"I'm sorry, sir, but you have to stay back," a young police officer ordered, standing firmly in Wade's way and arresting his progress.

"She's my…"

My what? he thought, unable to quantify their relationship properly but desperate to explain to the policeman that he had every right to be at her side when she was brought from the vehicle.

"Sir?"

"My girlfriend. She's my girlfriend," Wade repeated, as if doing so could get it through to the officer.

"There's nothing you can do right now. Just let the guys do their job. She'll be out in a minute or two."

"Is she all right? Do you know if she's hurt at all?" he asked, looking over the uniformed shoulder of the officer and trying anxiously to make out Piper's shape through the rain and the heavily coated fire rescue team.

To his infinite relief, he saw her moving and the instant the door was removed from the car, he watched as she was helped from the vehicle and to the waiting ambulance. One of the paramedics gestured for her to lie down on the gurney he had waiting but Wade felt a swell of pride as she shook her head and walked up the steps to the ambulance under her own steam.

"Can I go to her now, please?"

"Sure."

The officer stepped aside as Wade began to barge through. Given permission or not, nothing was going to stop him from checking on Piper himself. He bounded up the stairs of the ambulance, only to be barred at the top by one of the medics.

"I'm sorry, sir, but you can't—"

"It's okay, he's with me," Piper's voice came from inside the vehicle.

The man stepped aside to let Wade into the confined area. Piper sat on a gurney, a blood pressure cuff on one arm and a wad of dressing held to her nose. She pulled the dressing aside for a moment to speak.

"Don't worry, it's worse than it looks. The air bag gave me a bloody nose, that's all."

"Don't worry? Are you sure you're okay?"

"She'll have some seat belt bruising and be pretty sore the next few days but so far she checks out okay," the paramedic who was treating Piper said. He turned back to his patient. "Don't you want to go to the hospital just to be certain?"

"Yes, she does," Wade interjected. How could she know there weren't internal injuries? And besides, what if she was pregnant? What effect would the impact of the crash have had on the baby?

"No, I don't. Seriously. I'll be fine. I'm just a bit shaken up, that's all." Piper turned to Wade. "Please, I just want to go home and have a long soak in a warm bath right now."

"Is that wise?" Wade asked of the paramedic.

"Sure, just keep an eye on her. She doesn't appear to have a concussion or anything else serious."

"I'll do that. When can I take her home?"

"Just give us a few minutes to finalize our examination and take some details."

"Okay, I'll go and get my car."

Wade exited the ambulance and was relieved to see that traffic was being directed slowly and steadily past the accident scene. A tow truck was in the process of hoisting the wreck of Piper's car onto its flatbed.

"Are you the owner?" the tow truck driver asked Wade.

"Yes, I am."

"You were lucky, then."

"It wasn't me driving. It was my girlfriend."

Again that term that just didn't sit comfortably with him.

Piper was so different from that—less in some ways, but much more in others.

Wade looked at the damage to the vehicle. The passenger side had been entirely staved in. Had anyone been sitting there, they would probably be dead right now. He fought to control the ripple of fear that suffused him. Had the car hit the pole any differently, it could be Piper that was seriously injured, or worse. The car creaked and groaned in protest as the misshapen metal was hauled onto the truck. It was only once the driver was securing it with wide woven straps that Wade realized it had sustained rear end damage too, making him wonder what on earth had caused the crash in the first place.

"Do you know what happened?" he asked the tow truck driver.

"Cops think she was clipped by another driver, someone following too close and too fast, as she slowed for the corner. They shunted her across the road in a spin then took off. At least there were witnesses. They won't get away with it."

A red haze of fury swiftly replaced the fear that had earlier swamped him. A hit-and-run driver? If only he could get his hands on the lowlife scum, he'd teach them all about hit-and-run.

"So what do you want me to do with the wreck? I can take it to your home or to a panel beater of your choice so the insurance can get an assessor out. I doubt they'll do much but write it off, though."

"Just get rid of the thing."

"Are you sure, mate? You can sell the wreck for a couple hundred if you want."

"No, I never want to see it again," Wade said, his voice seething with tension. He reached into his pocket and took out a business card. "I don't give a damn what the insurance says. Just see to it that the towing bill and any disposal fees are sent to me and I'll take care of it."

"Whatever you say."

Wade waited a few minutes to cross the road and then jogged back to his car. Easing into the flow of traffic took some time and his fingers began drumming a rapid beat on the steering wheel. Eventually he managed to pull into a driveway near the ambulance.

He had to stifle his impatience a while longer as the police took a statement from Piper in the ambulance, getting from her as much detail about the incident as possible. Then, finally, he was allowed to take her home. The rain had slowed to a steady drizzle and the cold seeped through to his bones. But none of that mattered. Right now all he wanted was to get Piper home and to see for himself that she was okay. And then maybe to wrap her up in their bed and make sure nothing bad ever happened to her again.

His hands clenched into impotent fists at his side as he thought again about the driver who'd caused the accident. What he wouldn't do to have a bit of time alone with them right now.

Suddenly he could begin to understand why Rex hadn't wanted Piper to engage fully with the realities of the world. Why he'd wanted to keep his little girl safe in a fantasy world where nothing nasty ever happened to other people and where she didn't have to face unpleasantness. After losing his wife, was it really so surprising that the man had been determined to shield his only child? It might not have been the right thing for Piper, but it would have done a great deal toward soothing Rex's parental mind.

Transferring Piper into the car was accomplished with as much speed and efficiency as he could manage. She was already starting to feel the aftereffects of the crash and had begun to shake in reaction. He held open the passenger door of his car for her and leaned down to secure the seat belt across her body.

"Wade, I'm so sorry I smashed up the car."

"You're not to blame," he said tightly.

"But it's ruined, Wade. Did you see it? I know they say it wasn't my fault, but—"

"There are no buts. Just relax, we'll be home in a couple minutes and I'll get you into that bath you wanted."

Why the hell was she so upset about a car? Didn't she realize just how lucky she was not to have been more seriously hurt? And what about the whole reason she'd left work early in the first place?

"I'll need to get a ride with you to work tomorrow."

"Work can wait. I doubt you'll be up to it, anyway."

"But I don't have any sick leave," she protested.

"It's okay, I know your boss. Leave it with me."

Wade flashed her a tense smile even as his fingers gripped the steering wheel. He tried to order his thoughts. He had to ask her, he just had to.

"Piper," Wade said, fighting to keep his voice controlled and not to let any of his fear or worry cloud what he wanted to say. "Why did you leave work early?"

"I'll make up the time, don't worry," she said listlessly.

"Again, that's neither here nor there. One of the girls said you weren't feeling well."

"I must have had something for lunch that disagreed with me. It left me feeling off color and I couldn't concentrate on anything at work. I just wanted to head for bed. Fat lot of good that did me. I may as well have stayed at work."

"Are you sure it was something you ate?" he asked.

"Of course, what else..." Her words trailed off as understanding dawned. "Oh," she said, her voice suddenly very small and her face even paler than it had been before.

"Maybe we should get you checked at the hospital after all," Wade said.

"No, really, I don't want to go to the hospital, seriously."

"The doctor, then. Why don't I get May to come to the house?"

"Wade, I'll be fine. I've had an accident and I'm a bit shaken up and bruised. That's all. And if I am pregnant, there isn't anything we can do about it right now, anyway."

There was a fatalistic edge to her voice that he really didn't like but he could see she was adamant about not seeking medical advice just yet.

"Fine," he said, his jaw so tight he thought he might shatter teeth.

How could she be so cavalier? If she was carrying his child, he wanted an assurance that both she and the baby would be okay. Whether she liked it or not, he was calling May the moment he got Piper settled.

At the house, he helped Piper in through the back door where the warm and comforting smells of Mrs. Dexter's home cooking welcomed them.

"Oh, my, the two of you are wet through, and Miss Piper, is that blood under your nose? What on earth have you been up to?"

"Piper has been in an accident. She says she's fine and doesn't need a doctor, but would you take her upstairs and get her settled in a nice warm bath? She's going to need something soothing to offset the bruises she's earned today."

Wade tried to downplay the seriousness of the incident, his words earning him a grateful glance from Piper who allowed herself to succumb to Mrs. Dexter's fussing as the older woman led her from the room. The moment the women had gone upstairs, he took his cell phone from his pocket and dialed May Ritter's number.

"Dr. Ritter, please, it's urgent," he said as the receptionist took his call.

"Who's calling, please?"

Wade gritted his teeth as he replied, "Wade Collins."

"One moment, please."

The seriously hideous tones of prerecorded music filled his ears, doing nothing for his patience or his blood pressure.

"Wade, what's the problem?"

"Piper was in a car accident today and I think she might be pregnant. If she is, will the baby be okay?"

"Is she hurt?"

"Mostly shaken. The air bag gave her a bloody nose and the paramedic said she'll have bruising from the seat belt, too."

"Okay," May said soothingly. "So nothing too serious. What makes you think she's pregnant? She hasn't yet been in to see me again, or had any tests done."

"Aside from the obvious," he said, thinking about how they'd spent nearly all their nights since that first time back together, "she left work early today because she wasn't feeling well."

"Right," May answered.

He could hear the smile in her voice. It made him grip his phone all the more tightly in his hand. Didn't anyone understand how important this was?

"May," he growled.

"Okay, Wade, I know how much you want to be a dad. Look, the upside is that if she is pregnant, there is very little likelihood that anything has happened to the baby at this very early stage. Why don't you bring her in to see me tomorrow and we'll find out for certain if there is a baby, hmm?"

"Sure, thanks."

May gave him a time in the late morning and Wade hung up from the call feeling minutely better than he had at the start of it. She said he had nothing to worry about. So why did he feel as if his entire world was under threat?

Mrs. Dexter came back into the kitchen.

"I'll put together a tray for Miss Piper, something she can eat cold when she feels like it. I don't think she'll be up to much for dinner tonight. That crash has left her quite upset."

"Was she okay when you left her?"

"She was just getting into the bath. Poor girl, she can't seem to stop shaking."

"It'll be shock setting in. She was very calm at the scene, too calm probably. Can you make that tray for two? And when it's ready, perhaps you could leave it in my sitting room. I'll go up and see to her now."

Wade ascended the stairs two at a time. For his own peace of mind he needed to see Piper was okay. As he entered his bedroom, the fragrant scent of bath crystals came from the open en suite bathroom doorway. A small sound caught his ear, a sound that made every muscle in his body tense. Piper was crying.

He was at her side in seconds.

"Are you okay? Should I call an ambulance?"

"N-no, I'm okay. I just can't stop. I keep going through it in my mind, seeing that post coming toward me and feeling the helplessness all over again."

Tremors shook her frame making ripples on the water. Wade didn't think twice. It took only a moment to shuck off his clothes and shoes and to slide into the giant old tub behind her. He pulled her against his chest and wrapped his arms around her, holding her secure, and propping her head against his shoulder. From this angle he could see the dark angry-looking bruise that was coming out on her skin. His anger against the driver who caused the accident warred with intense relief that she had not been seriously injured. The tumult of emotions was foreign to him. Usually he had no difficulty in keeping his feelings in check, in separating logic from sentiment. But there was something about Piper that scrambled all reason.

"There," he said quietly, "does that feel better?"

She nodded, the soft curls that clouded her head tickling the side of his neck as she did so. Her hair had grown in the past six weeks from the somewhat haphazard pixie cut she'd shorn it into when she'd gotten rid of her dreadlocks.

The shorter hair had suited her, emphasizing her fine bone structure and the slenderness of her elegant neck, but he preferred this slightly softer look. The lack of structure gave her a femininity that appealed directly to his core every time he looked her way.

Wade relaxed against the porcelain and let his eyes slide closed, relishing the sense of rightness that infused him as he held Piper in his arms. If only it could always be this easy to keep a loved one safe.

His eyes flew open and his hold on her tightened. Loved one? Had he done the impossible and fallen in love with Piper all over again? No, he couldn't have. What he felt right now was his own aftermath of shock. He was concerned about her. Of course he was, she might be pregnant with his baby and she had been at terrible risk today. It was his duty to look after her. To keep her safe. That's all.

She nestled a little closer, and his arms tightened automatically in response. No, he didn't love her. He couldn't.

But that didn't mean he was planning to let go any time soon, either.

Twelve

Piper relaxed against him in the delicious warm water, the sobs that shook her slowly easing, her tremors finally going away altogether. It was as if by his very presence Wade drew all that reaction and upset away and exiled it where it could no longer affect her.

Her hands rested over her belly, Wade's resting over hers. For the first moment in a very long time, Piper felt one-hundred-percent safe.

Today had been one out of the bag. She hadn't been feeling all that great when she'd risen in the morning but some toast and tea at breakfast had taken care of that. She'd hoped that lunch would improve how she'd felt again later in the morning, but instead it had left her feeling much worse.

Her mind circled the prospect that Wade had raised. Could she be pregnant already? It would be pretty soon by any standards but then again some people were lucky enough, or unlucky enough, to fall pregnant right away. Hadn't it been that way with her and Wade to begin with?

Through the whole of their relationship eight years prior, the lovemaking had been passionate and thoroughly satisfying. And yet, she'd always held something back—afraid to let herself give in to the powerful emotions he made her feel. She'd always felt she couldn't let him in all the way until she was truly certain of his love.

Then she'd made the play to win him away from her father's influence, and she'd pulled out the big guns. It had been weeks since they'd made love. Plus, things had gotten so tense between her and Rex that she'd made up her mind to leave. Wade, caught in the middle between the two Mitchells, had gotten frustrated with both of them, leading to endless arguments with Piper that had served to destroy any passion between them. Wade had extended an olive branch in an attempt to make up and during a romantic evening at the scummy flat he was living in, she'd given him her all. She'd let herself love him completely, had given up her heart and soul along with her body to him in complete abandon.

In the morning, when they'd woken, she'd assumed he would prove that he returned her love by going along with her plan to leave New Zealand behind. After all, hadn't they both just had the most amazing night of their lives? Didn't he love her enough to come with her when she left? Apparently not.

She still couldn't believe she'd been so stupid, so naive even, to have thought that she could tempt a man like Wade with what she'd had to offer him back then. Yes, she'd loved him, but what kind of life could she have given him? He was a smart, ambitious man, and she'd tried to get him to give up all his prospects for a role as her arm candy while she traveled the world. He never would have been happy with a purposeless life like that. Truth be told, she hadn't been happy with it, either. Not that she was willing to admit that—especially at first. She had tried to tell herself that she was better off without a man who would let her go after a night like the one they'd shared.

Of course, finding out she was pregnant as a result of that night together she'd seen as some kind of karmic retribution for her behavior. And then losing that baby had been harder to deal with than she'd ever anticipated. She'd never expected to want a child, or to love it. And she'd never realized what a massive hole it would leave in her life when it was gone. She'd gone back to partying afterward, trying to numb the pain, but that was her first step in really growing up.

Now she felt—hoped—that she'd left that selfish past behind her. But what did the future hold? She may already be pregnant, again. With Wade's child, again. A child conceived again in love on her part...but not on his. Could their story have a happier ending this time?

Wade stirred, lifting one foot to toe open the faucet and run some more hot water into the bath. She hadn't even noticed the water had cooled.

"Another ten minutes and then I think we should get out, okay?"

"Sure, the wrinkled prune look really isn't my best."

She felt him turn slightly and press a kiss to the top of her head.

"I can think of better," he murmured.

Piper leaned forward and turned off the running water. Aside from a few aches and pains, most of them centered from the pressure marks across her chest, she felt a whole lot better now. So much so, that when she leaned back against Wade, and discovered a vital part of him was also feeling pretty darn good, it was a simple matter to roll over and place her knees on either side of his legs.

"Hey, aren't you supposed to be resting?"

"I feel fine," she said, even as shifting her body made her wince a little.

"Fine, huh? Doesn't look like it to me. Piper, we don't have to—"

"I want to, Wade. I want you. I want to make love to you and make all the bad stuff go away."

Wade skimmed his hands up and down her arms lightly. "And will it go away?"

"Let's find out, shall we?"

She leaned forward and kissed him, a hot, wet kiss that sent a slow beat thrumming through her veins. Her hands slicked across his shoulders and she relished the vital strength of him. She'd never been more grateful for life than she was at this very moment. The accident had been surreal, the aftermath even more so. But this, this was something quantifiable, something valid and true.

The man beneath her had given her second chances, and with them had shown her a generosity she'd never expected, despite their very rocky start. But now, the reality of making up to him all that she'd destroyed so long ago was completely within her grasp. And it wasn't all that was within her grasp, she acknowledged as the blunt tip of him nudged against her lower belly. She lifted her hips and used one hand to position him at her entrance before slowly and carefully lowering herself until he was buried within her. Deep inside she felt the flex of his hardened length and she rocked gently against him.

Sensation built within her in steady waves as she continued to move. Wade's hands gripped her hips, his fingers taut against her skin. His eyes met and locked with hers, silently urging her on, glazing with desire as she let her hips undulate back and forth.

Water sloshed against the high sides of the bath, every now and then spilling over the side and onto the tiled floor, but she didn't care. Not when every nerve in her body was centered on the point where their bodies joined. Not when her body felt so aflame that she thought the water about them might boil off. Wade raised his head and captured one of her nipples with his mouth, his lips sealing around the tightened aureole and his teeth lightly scraping the extended tip.

A spear of heat shot directly from her breast to her core and as Wade began to suckle the rigid bud, her orgasm began to creep over her—at first a gentle swell of pleasure, but rapidly culminating in a crash of sensation that made spots swim in her vision and her body shake with its force.

She collapsed against him, even as he thrust upward, lost in the glory of his own climax. Both were oblivious to all but the passion that spent itself in tiny aftershocks that made them shudder against one another. Each clench of her body triggering another with him, each flex of his erection setting off a chain reaction that tingled all the way to her extremities.

"I didn't think it could get any better between us," she panted against his shoulder.

In response Wade wrapped his arms around her waist and held her close to him. They were each obviously as reluctant as the other to relinquish the closeness, the sheer perfection of physical pleasure they'd achieved together but, after some time, the cooling water about them became sufficient incentive to pull apart and get out of the bath.

Wade wrapped one of the big thick bath towels from the heated rail around his waist before using the other to dry Piper with gentle strokes. Under his careful ministrations she unexpectedly felt ridiculously emotional. She bit her lower lip to hold back the sob that built deep inside. Wade looked at her, worry drawing his brows together in a straight line.

"Did I hurt you?"

"No, I'm just still a bit of a mess, I think."

"It's okay," he said, reaching for one of the large fluffy bathrobes on the hook behind the bathroom door and helping her into it. "It's been quite a day, hmm?"

She nodded. Unable to speak for fear that she'd blurt out her feelings for him and ruin everything. Right now she had a deep-seated need for his undivided attention and she wasn't prepared to do anything to jeopardize that.

"Let's have something to eat. Mrs. Dexter was going to leave a tray in the sitting room for us."

He wiped an errant tear from her cheek then took her hand and led her to the sitting room. A cheerful fire danced in the fireplace behind the screen and someone, no doubt Mrs. Dexter, had drawn the drapes and switched on a pair of table lamps that cast a gentle glow about the room. Weariness seeped through her, making her feel lethargic and uncoordinated. She sank gratefully onto one of the sofas by the fireplace as Wade inspected the contents of the tray.

"Here," he said, smoothing some red paste onto a sliver of sliced French bread and passing it over to her.

Piper felt some of her lethargy dispel as the piquant flavor hit her tongue. "Mmm, that's delicious. What is it?"

"I think it's a sundried tomato hummus. Want some more?"

"Try and hold me back," she answered.

Together they ate their way through the selection of food, enjoying the cold roasted chicken drumsticks that had been coated with Dexie's special herb flavoring, licking one another's fingers clean and savoring the variety of finger foods that had been laid out for them. They eschewed the bottle of wine that sat in a frosted cooler, enjoying instead the mineral water that came from the small fridge that Wade had integrated into a wall unit along one side of the sitting room.

Finally replete, Piper curled up her legs under her and rested her head against the back of the sofa.

"Tired?" Wade asked.

"Yeah, shattered actually."

"Why don't you go to bed?"

"It's still so early," she protested even as she fought off a yawn.

"No one is going to blame you. You had a major fright

today, and you haven't been feeling well." He hesitated and drew in a breath before continuing. "I've made an appointment for you to see May tomorrow morning."

She swung her legs down and sat upright. "I told you, I'm okay. Why did you do that?"

"I need to be sure, Piper."

"Can't we just see how I'm feeling tomorrow?"

"You had to leave work because you weren't well, don't you want to find out why?"

"Whatever it was, it's passed now. I feel tired and a bit sore from the accident, but aside from that I'm okay. I really don't want to go to May tomorrow. Shouldn't that be up to me, anyway?"

Wade gave her another piercing look. "What is it that you're afraid of, Piper?"

He narrowed his eyes as he looked at her and she felt her defenses rise. She knew how much he wanted her to be pregnant, but what would happen next if she was? The prospect terrified her. She wouldn't be alone as she had been the last time she'd found out she was pregnant, but would he still want her in his bed each night once he'd achieved his objective? Or would she be tucked away, left to procreate under the clinical terms of their agreement?

She loved him. She wanted to be with him. She knew he didn't love her, but the longer she could put off him having a reason to set her aside, the better her chance of breaking through the shell he operated within. The better her chance of possibly creating a mutual affection between them that might stand the test of time. That would see them raise their child together, in a home filled with love.

"I'm not afraid. I just don't see the need, that's all," she hedged. "It's not as if I've missed a period or anything like that."

"And yet you must be feeling some changes in your body. Your breasts are slightly fuller, are they not?" He pushed aside the neckline of her robe, revealing her breasts to his glittering gaze. One finger brushed across their pink tips making them instantly taut and her insides coil tight. "And are your nipples not more sensitive than before?"

She shoved his hand away from her, even as her blood heated again in her body. Pulling her robe closed, she got up from the sofa and went to stand in front of the fire.

"That doesn't mean anything," she answered defiantly. "You're a fantastic lover, maybe it's just my reaction to you."

Wade stood and came right up to her, his hand sliding inside her robe once more, this time to rest against her lower stomach. "Or your body's natural reaction to our lovemaking—our *baby* making."

"Wade—"

"I'll pick you up at ten-thirty tomorrow, your appointment is for eleven. You will keep it, Piper. As I said before, I *need* to know."

Piper felt a stab of loss at his words. Finding out if she was pregnant or not was all that mattered to him now.

"What about work?"

"Like I said, I don't think you'll feel up to going into the office tomorrow."

"Shouldn't I be the judge of that?"

Wade sighed in frustration. "Look, you're not going to win this argument, Piper. You will see May tomorrow and that's final. Whether you go to work or not is up to you entirely, although I'd advise against it."

He turned and stalked to the bedroom, reappearing a few minutes later dressed casually in a pair of jeans and a turtlenecked sweater that made him look altogether too sexy for words. Even as angry and frustrated as she was with his high-handedness, she still wanted him on a level she'd never known before. The knowledge frightened her about as much as the prospect that she might be carrying his baby and be about to be shelved until the *happy* event.

"Go to bed, Piper. You're just about dead on your feet. I'll be downstairs catching up on some work."

He picked up the tray with their plates and leftovers and took it from the room, leaving her alone with only the sound of the fire crackling behind her as company. The instant he was gone, Piper felt every last vestige of fight leave her body. Okay, so she'd go to bed now. But it would be because she wanted to and because she was tired. Not because she'd been summarily ordered to.

Despite her weariness, sleep remained elusive until she heard Wade return upstairs several hours later. Through the open bedroom door she heard the clink of crystal as he poured himself a glass of port, then his deep sigh as he settled onto one of the chairs. It was another half hour before he quietly entered the bathroom, and a few more minutes before he then, finally, slid into the bed beside her, his naked body spooning hers, his arms coming around her in their usual nightly embrace, one hand gently cupping her left breast.

Only then did she slide into a deep slumber, her body relaxed against his warmth, her heart in his hands.

Wade waited in the reception area at the doctor's office with increasing impatience. Piper had been in May's consulting room for over half an hour now and the length of time she'd been gone was driving him crazy. How long did it take to do a pregnancy test, anyway? Maybe he should have conceded to Piper's wish not to come to the doctor today, but made her do a test at home instead.

"Mr. Collins?"

He shot to his feet as the receptionist called his name. "Yes?"

"Dr. Ritter would like you to go through now." The woman gestured down the passageway leading from the waiting area. "Second to last door on the right."

"Thanks," he said, even as his feet began to eat up the distance between torment and the answers he sought.

He tapped lightly on the door and opened it on May's command to enter. Wade's gaze flicked from one woman to the other, but he could read nothing on their faces. Piper's expression remained completely empty. Mind you, she'd been quiet this morning—her movements stiff as a result of yesterday's trauma. May, too, kept her features inscrutable but she gestured to him to take a seat next to Piper.

"I'm sure you know by now that there are no long-term issues with the minor injuries that Piper sustained in her accident yesterday," May said. "However, she will need to be very careful for the next few months."

Wade's heart leaped in his chest. "The next few months?" he repeated.

"Yes, indeed."

"So does that mean...?" He was suddenly too afraid to enunciate the words in case it might not be true.

May smiled. "Yes, you two are expecting a baby, congratulations."

Wade sat back in his chair, filled with emotion, filled with hope. Could it be that his dreams were finally coming true? And if so, why did Piper now look so stricken?

Thirteen

She was pregnant. Numbness invaded every cell in her body. When May had confirmed the result of the urine test to her, Piper had retreated behind a wall of denial. All through her physical examination she'd been in another place. A place that froze her in fear. After the confirmation, she'd asked May what was the likelihood of her miscarrying again. The answer was about as indeterminate as the wispy drifts of fog that had surrounded the house this morning.

Without knowing what had caused her to miscarry the first time, May couldn't give her any promises.

Piper slid a glance at Wade. He was ecstatic. His face glowed with the light of sheer joy. It terrified her. What if she let him down? What if she couldn't carry this baby to term?

She vaguely heard May and Wade discussing what happened next, the list of appointments she'd need to attend, when she'd have scans, etc. The words flew over her head. Wade could take care of that. Right now those matters were the least of her worries. Learning how to cope with the crippling fear that held her frozen in her seat was going to be the biggest thing for her right now.

On the ride home from the doctor's office, Wade exuded a different energy. His conversation concentrated solely on the baby they now knew she carried. Her stomach flipped uncomfortably.

"Stop the car!" she cried.

"Stop?"

"Now!"

Wade pulled over to the curb. Before the car was fully stationary Piper flung open her door and struggled to her feet. Every muscle in her body ached today and moving was difficult. She made it to a tree on the grassy verge and leaned both arms against it, dropping her head down between her shoulders and dragging in big gulps of the chill, damp air.

How was she going to get through this if Wade talking about the baby was enough to made her nauseous?

She felt his hand at the nape of her neck, his fingers stroking gently.

"You okay?"

"No," she answered with a shaky voice. She was most definitely not okay.

"Take your time," he said considerately.

"Yeah, I'll do that."

Wade continued the gentle stroking and Piper focused on the sensation of his skin on hers. His warmth versus the chill that consumed her. Finally her stomach settled and the threat of being ill diminished.

"I think we can go now," she said, straightening up from the tree and squaring her shoulders.

"Are you sure? We don't need to hurry."

Again that consideration. If she hadn't been pregnant, would he have been so solicitous?

"I'm fine. Can we go home now, please?"

Wade's hand drifted down her spine, resting at her lower

back as they walked to the car. He saw her settled in the passenger seat and leaned down to clip her seat belt across her. She flinched as he did so, her bruise now a painful reminder of her date with the lamp post yesterday.

"Sorry," Wade said.

"It's okay, I'm not going to break, you know."

"No, but you do need special care and attention."

He leaned one arm across the top of the doorway to the car and looked down at her.

"Why? Just because I'm pregnant?" She couldn't help it, the words sprang forth before she could hold them back.

"That and because of what you've been through. Cut me some slack, okay, Piper. Let me take care of you. Anyone can see the news has come as a bit of a shock to you. I have to admit that I'm a little overwhelmed myself. I never thought we'd get it right so quickly."

He closed the door and walked around the front of the car toward the driver's side. Piper stared out the windshield. Get it right? If that was the case, why did she feel as if everything was going so very wrong? She felt as if things were spinning out of her control. She'd expected—no, *wanted*—to have time to win Wade over, woo him back to her. Now, she was afraid his primary thought would only be for their son or daughter. She wouldn't matter as much to him as he mattered to her.

She knew exactly where she stood under the terms of their contract—for as long as she stayed under his roof at least. But how could she continue to do that, loving him the way she did, when his whole focus would be on the baby? Where would she fit in once the baby was born? Would he still want her? And what if the worst happened again? What if she miscarried? Would he believe her when she said she'd loved this child from the point of its conception, that she loved its father just as much?

* * *

The weeks seemed to race by. Wade consulted one of the baby books he'd bought and kept at work, that showed the varying stages of pregnancy and development of the fetus, fascinated by every step. Piper was fourteen weeks now and while she was still as slender as always, there was a tautness to her lower belly that hadn't been there before and her breasts had filled out, too, and continued to be highly sensitive—a fact he'd delighted in exploring when they made love.

He frowned as he considered the terminology—making love. It had been sex when it started but somewhere along the line his feelings about the act itself had changed. Who was he kidding? His feelings about Piper were changing. Especially now. He knew he was becoming more possessive and protective of her with every day that passed—even to the point that he'd soundly rejected her suggestion that now she was pregnant she move back to her old room. She and the baby were his to take care of—and he was starting to wonder if he wasn't doing a good enough job.

She'd been fragile when she'd returned from overseas but she seemed even more brittle now. As if she might shatter into a million tiny shards if the wind so much as blew the wrong way. Personally, he felt she'd taken on too much. She still worked her full days at Mitchell Exports and spent her evening hours studying or attending late classes for the pre-entry course she'd insisted on completing.

"I have to finish something in my life," she'd snapped when he'd suggested perhaps she could leave the papers since it was putting so much strain on her.

He'd been taken aback at her response, but had left her to it. She hadn't wanted her colleagues at work to know about her pregnancy, insisting it was her and Wade's business and no one else's. He'd felt the complete opposite, he wanted to shout their news from the rooftops. Even so, he'd respected her decision and remained silent on the subject, except for letting her immediate superiors know and informing them that he expected her workload to lighten somewhat. They'd been only too happy to accommodate his request, even while expressing their surprise at her condition because no one in the office, aside from his PA, had been let into the truth of their relationship.

Perhaps he'd let the cat out of the bag about the two of them prematurely, he thought. Piper obviously had her reasons for wanting to keep their relationship quiet—although they wouldn't be able to do that for much longer—and for asserting her independence. As to the latter, she had barely blinked when he'd arranged for delivery of an Audi A5 for her. Wade had elaborated on the safety features of the car including antilock electronic braking, traction control and the number of air bags. She'd merely accepted the keys and driven off as usual.

Nothing seemed to break through the mantle of eerie calm that enveloped her. The only time she showed any genuine emotion or response was when they were in bed. Even then, she was often so exhausted when she came to bed that she'd fall immediately asleep.

He'd expected some animation from her when he'd discussed redecorating the nursery, but she'd quietly agreed with every suggestion he had made and appeared quite happy to allow the interior designer he'd appointed a free hand. The decorator was supposed to be finished today. He was keen to see the final result and rued that he wouldn't be able to see it together with Piper for the first time. He'd hoped the completed room would imbue some excitement about the baby into her.

It was late when he arrived home and his stomach was growling with hunger. Despite that, Wade ignored the plate he knew Mrs. Dexter would have left in the oven for him and shot up the stairs to the next floor. When he'd walked from the garage to the house he'd seen a light on upstairs, in the nursery. He hoped it meant that Piper was in there.

The scents of new wallpaper, carpet and fresh paint filled the corridor outside the room as he approached. The door swung lightly open at his touch. A surge of satisfaction swelled inside as he saw Piper standing by the pale wooden tallboy, with her back to the door. One drawer stood open and it looked as if she was holding an item of clothing.

"They've done a great job with the room, don't you think?" he asked as he entered, his critical eye scanning the room and finding not a single thing at fault.

"Yes," Piper answered, her voice sounding thick and strained.

"Piper? What's wrong? Is it the baby?"

Wade stepped up to her, placed a gentle hand on her shoulder and turned her to face him. It stunned him to see abject misery painted on her features, her face wet with the tears that rolled off her lashes and down her cheeks.

She shook her head and moved away. He noticed the way her hands grasped the tiny one-piece suit in her hands, her knuckles white with the intensity of her grip.

"What is then?" he asked, confused. "Is it hormones?"

She sniffed a stifled laugh. "No, Wade, it's not hormones. I just…"

"You just, what?" he prompted when she didn't continue.

She lifted her face toward his, her blue eyes glittering behind the moisture there.

"I don't know how I'm going to go through with this."

"This?" he asked, a steel fist tightening around his lungs and making it almost impossible to draw breath.

What was she talking about?

"This," she said, gesturing to the room. "The baby, being a mother, all of it. I just don't think I can do it."

She couldn't do it? What the hell was she suggesting? A termination? Over his dead body. Anger rose swift and fast.

Had this been her plan all along? And to think he'd started to believe he loved her!

"You can do it and you will," he said in a voice that was barely controlled.

"There are so many things that are out of my control, I'm terrified," she sobbed. "Wade, you don't understand—"

"Understand? Oh, yes, I think I understand all right. The first sign of anything you might have to do the hard way and you run, don't you, Piper? Just like you ran before. Well, I have news for you and it goes like this. You *will* continue with this pregnancy and you *will* have this baby."

Piper looked at him with an expression akin to horror in her eyes. "But what if something happens?" she implored.

"Happens? What? Like last time? Don't think you're going to terminate my baby again, Piper. I might not have been able to prevent you from killing my son or daughter eight years ago but you can rest assured that even if I have to lock you in your room, you will most definitely bring this child to term."

Piper felt all the blood drain from her face and she swayed a little with dizziness. *He knew?*

"How did you find out?" she whispered, her throat closing on the words.

"That's totally irrelevant. The thing is that I did. You know, I really thought you were proving that you were capable of being a decent person, someone who was reliable and honest, but you just haven't changed one bit, have you? You're incapable of growing up, of taking or accepting responsibility. Well, understand this, if anything, and I mean *anything,* happens to this baby, I will hold you fully accountable and I will hunt you to the ends of the earth to make you pay."

Piper recoiled, feeling each one of his words as if it was a physical blow. She wanted to protest, but she couldn't. The words jammed in her throat. It was all she could do right now to hold on to consciousness. She dragged in a ragged breath.

"You make it sound like it was all my fault," she finally managed.

Wade shot her a look of pure venom. "Wasn't it?"

"No!" she cried. "It wasn't, how could it have been?"

"I don't believe you, Piper."

"You don't believe me?"

How could he not? She hadn't done anything to cause the miscarriage of that baby, and the loss still weighed upon her as heavily today as it had back then. Perhaps even more so. Piper's heart hammered in her chest. She couldn't believe this conversation was happening. How had he ever found out? And, even more importantly, how long ago? She forced down the fear and the shock that threatened to take over her before speaking.

"How did you find out?"

"That isn't important. What's important is that I will not let something like that ever happen again to a child of mine."

The possessive tone of his voice reverberated right through her. Here he was, claiming ownership to a child he'd never known. It catalyzed a spur of anger of her own.

"A child of yours. And what makes you so sure that it was?"

He paled before her, two deep lines bracketing his mouth as his jaw assumed a grim set.

"Are you saying it wasn't?"

"I'm not saying anything. I never did say anything. That's the point. How the hell did you know about it?"

"Rex told me. He came to work one morning an absolute wreck. He told me that you'd aborted. He never put two and two together. He never suspected it was my baby he was talking about." Wade brushed his eyes with one hand. "Do you have any idea what that did to me? I'm not a fool. While your father never would have thought to do the math, I knew. I *knew* it was my child he was talking about. The child you never told me about. How could you have done such a thing?"

How could he *believe* she would do such a thing? The question rattled through her mind. She'd loved him. She'd thought he loved her, *understood* her. They'd shared some bitter words when they'd parted but he still had to have known that deep down she would never willingly take a life.

"But I didn't do anything. I lost the baby. It was a miscarriage—I had no control over what happened. None."

"And you expect me to believe you?"

"Yes, of course I do. I'm telling you the truth."

"And you're such an advocate of honesty, aren't you? You once told me that you loved me and we both know that was a lie. Of course I don't believe you. Your father had nothing to gain by lying to me. You, however…"

He let his voice trail away and Piper knew without a shadow of a doubt that she stood no chance of swaying his belief. Deep inside, the hope that she and Wade could make something of this together shriveled and died. There was no way they could ever have a future together.

"Knowing how you feel about me, I'm amazed you could bring yourself to have sex with me."

The words tasted like ashes in her mouth. Sex? For her every intimate moment had been a silent expression of love. But clearly he'd had his own agenda all along. She'd been a complete fool to believe otherwise. A new thought bloomed in her mind.

"Is that why you loaned that money to my trust fund? So you'd have leverage over me?"

"You owed me, Piper. Big time."

"You planned this all along?" She shook her head in disbelief. "How could you? How could you harbor so much bitterness and anger toward me for so long?"

"How?" he answered. "Easy. I want what you took from me, what you denied me the right to. A few hundred thousand dollars? That's nothing. But you know that, don't you? You always treated money as nothing. To you it was merely a means to an end, not something to be earned or revered in any form. But a life? Not even you have the right to deem that as dispensable. Just think of this as a means to an end. That, at least, is something you should understand."

"It wasn't my fault," she said softly. "Please believe me, Wade. There isn't a day that goes by that I don't regret the choices I made. I've spent years trying to make that up. It's why I came home. I know I did you wrong when I left. I know I hurt my father. I wanted to make it right."

"Well, now you have the perfect opportunity, don't you?" Wade said, his words like shards of ice. "Have this baby and then move on."

Fourteen

Move on? Like she could just have this baby, a child that was flesh of her flesh, heart of her heart, and then leave? She stared at Wade in shock.

"But you said that it was my choice. To stay and be a part of our baby's upbringing or not."

"I've changed my mind," he said. "Once the baby is here I want you gone. My child deserves the right to be able to trust the people around him or her. He doesn't deserve people who will mouth platitudes when it suits them then leave the second the going gets tough."

"And you think I'd do that?"

He raised a cynical brow. "Your track record precedes you."

"I've changed, Wade. I've learned the difference between what's right and what's wrong. I've learned to value the people that matter."

"Pretty words, Piper. You were always so very good at them." He turned to leave the nursery but at the door he hesitated. "I think it would be best, under the circumstances, if you moved back into your own room tonight. I'll see to it that your things are transferred over tomorrow."

Wade lay in his bed, staring at the shadows of the molded plaster ceiling above him and missing Piper's presence by his side with a physical ache. He'd thought she'd changed, but she hadn't, and the knowledge hurt far more than he could ever have anticipated. He felt like such an idiot. He'd believed she wanted to change, to make a step forward in the right direction but she'd fooled him yet again. He thought he'd inured himself to the harm she could wreak but he'd been a lightweight in the face of everything. He couldn't afford to let her close again. If she could do this to him, what emotional hurt might she be capable of inflicting on their baby? A fierce surge of protectiveness toward his unborn child suffused him, masking the pain that dwelt deep inside. Piper was just like his father had been, paying lip service to what he wanted to hear and then letting him down yet again.

It hadn't been so bad while his mother was alive, or at least he hadn't noticed it so much with the buffer of her love there between him and his old man. But when she'd died unexpectedly, Eric Collins had been exposed for the sham he was. He'd downright refused to care for his ten-year-old son, and while Wade had bravely battled on, on his own in the house he'd been raised in, it hadn't taken long for neighbors to notice his father's absence and Social Services had been called in.

He could still hear his father's lies on the afternoon he'd been taken away, one of the rare days his father had actually been home—this time smelling of a rank combination of alcohol and stale perfume.

"I'm sorry, son," he'd said. "You know I'd keep you if I could. I'll come for you, I promise."

But Wade had recognized the look in his father's eyes,

heard the words for the platitudes they were. The look that told him his father was lying through his teeth. Wade knew that Eric Collins had no intention of ever trying to get his son back and that he couldn't wait to be free of him. It made the loss of his mother all the more painful.

Being fostered hadn't been so bad. The couple who'd cared for him were decent folk with strict rules. He'd learned that as long as he didn't rock the boat, life was pretty straightforward. But every night as he lay in the narrow bunk bed in a room with three other boys, he'd made a promise that he would always be there for any child of his. Always. No matter what.

The fact he hadn't had the chance to be there for his first baby was a scar he'd bear on his heart for all his days. But with this baby, everything would be different. And Piper Mitchell would just have to get used to the idea.

The next few days proved uncomfortable between them. At least at work Wade could lose himself in the day-to-day business that filled his time, only needing to cross paths with Piper when absolutely necessary. That wasn't to say he didn't keep a wary eye on her activity. Her movements in and out the office were carefully monitored. He didn't trust her, not one inch.

At home it was more difficult to keep his distance. He'd taken to bringing work home and eating his meals in the library. Fielding the looks of concern from Dexter and his wife became a daily chore. He hated the atmosphere that hung around the place but, he consoled himself, it wouldn't be forever. Once the baby was born and Piper had gone on to whatever it was that she wanted to do next, life would be much sweeter.

He ignored the pang of regret at the thought of Piper leaving and reminded himself that she'd done it before, she would just as easily do so again. Except this time, she wouldn't be taking his child with her.

It was two weeks after things had come to a head that

Wade faced a difficult choice. The senior manager in one of his new Pacific Island outstations had suffered a mild stroke. Most of the staff in the office had only been there a few months, and none were in a position to step in and assume a temporary management role. The one guy he could send from the Auckland office, Roy Beckett, was in Europe on other business and it was vital that Roy conclude the contract negotiations in person. It would be four days before Roy was able to travel back and pick up the reins in Samoa.

That left only one alternative, that Wade go there himself. The thought of leaving Piper behind made his stomach clench, but he didn't like the idea of her traveling with him, either. She looked so fragile these days, with a strain around her eyes giving her a haunted look that had everyone in her department constantly asking if she was okay. Here, at the house, Mrs. Dexter was like a mother hen clucking around her chick. Making sure Piper had small nutritious meals and that she did nothing more taxing than lift a cup of tea.

Surely, with so many people looking out for her, she wouldn't do anything stupid. Wade leaned back in his chair and rubbed his eyes wearily. She was sixteen weeks. The books told him that she may have felt movement by now. He couldn't imagine that even she would be able to bring herself to source a termination now.

He was in an untenable position. He had to go, but everything in him screamed not to. There was nothing else for it but to get to Samoa and back as quickly as he could. He put in a call to Roy and explained the situation. Roy assured him he could be in Samoa by Sunday. Today was Tuesday. Wade thanked him and hung up before lifting the receiver and dialing the airline. The sooner he got this sorted, the sooner he'd be home.

Piper missed Wade. Until this morning, he'd barely spoken a dozen words to her since that awful night. She'd come down to breakfast only to find him at the kitchen table, waiting for her. She didn't bother to hide her surprise. That he'd been actively avoiding her hadn't gone unnoticed. Frankly, it only served to make her even more tense as she found herself continually anticipating the moments their paths would cross. At least this face-to-face situation was something she could handle. She'd learned during her aid work that things were best faced head-on. But what was a girl to do when the person she had to face refused to believe her?

Wade stood as she came into the kitchen, scraping his chair back across the polished wooden floor. Mrs. Dexter flung a look from one to the other and grabbed a dusting cloth.

"I'll be in the morning room if you need me," she said, bustling past.

As soon as the door swung shut behind her, Wade spoke, "I have to go away for a few days."

"Away?"

That was the last thing she'd been expecting. While he'd kept his distance from her, she knew full well that he was aware of everything she did. It was suffocating, but there was nothing she could do about it.

"A situation has arisen in our office in Apia. I'll be back on Monday."

"Nothing too serious, I hope," she said neutrally.

She was well aware that the Apia office was still in a fledgling state. A serious disruption could see a major setback in operations. And it had to be serious if Wade, himself, was going.

"James, the manager there, has had a stroke. He's going to be okay but it'll be some time before he's up to speed again. Roy is coming through to relieve him on his way back from Europe, but someone needs to run things until he arrives. No one in the office already is qualified to handle it."

"And there's no one else who can go?"

"Do you think I'd be going if I had any alternative?"

She shook her head.

Wade continued, "My flight leaves this afternoon. I'll be leaving my car at the airport."

"Are you sure you want to do that? I could always take you."

"No, my return flight doesn't get in until nearly midnight on Monday."

She experienced a fleeting gratefulness that she wouldn't have to stay awake until then. Most evenings she was in bed by nine-thirty these days. Long gone were late nights, that was for sure. But she'd have done it, for him.

"Well, if you're sure," she said.

"I am. And Piper?"

She looked up, meeting his eyes for the first time in what felt like forever.

"Do not do anything you might regret while I'm gone."

"What do you mean?"

"You know exactly what I mean," he said, a thread of anger tingeing his words.

She put a protective hand to her belly, feeling the slight swelling there.

"I wouldn't do anything to hurt my baby. Not now, and not in the past. Why don't you believe me on that?"

He didn't answer immediately, then his shoulders seemed to sag beneath the fine wool of his tailored suit.

"I want to believe you, Piper, but history has a way of repeating itself and, to be frank, I don't trust you."

She reached forward, putting a hand on his forearm, absorbing the heat of him through his clothing and feeling that old familiar tingle of awareness.

"You can trust me."

"I wish I could be certain of that."

"What do I have to do to make you believe me?"

He shook his head. "I don't know. I used to think a person's word meant something, but I learned a long time ago that words are only any good when they're backed up by actions."

"You're talking about your father, aren't you? I'm not like him, Wade. I'm not."

He recoiled at her words, pulling his arm out from under her touch.

"I'm leaving straight from the office. Just do as I ask, Piper, and don't do anything stupid."

Without another word, or a backward glance, he left the kitchen. She stood there, hurt beyond belief at his words. He was a closed book, a story stubbornly unwilling to be rewritten. She went through the motions of eating breakfast, not out of any hunger but because she knew she had to provide the very best of everything for the child growing inside her. This time she had to get it right.

The house was quiet when she arrived home from work on Friday night. The Dexters were using their night off to see a live show in the city and there was a note in the kitchen with instructions for Piper to reheat her meal. She smiled at the neatly handwritten bullet-pointed note. Did Dexie not think she was even capable of reheating a meal on her own?

She shook her head, then flinched as the headache she'd been suffering from most of the day sharpened. She was reluctant to take anything for it, but if it continued to worsen she'd have to try something. A shiver ran through her. She'd felt the cold far more than usual today, and she decided to forgo dinner for now in lieu of getting on some warmer clothes.

Upstairs in her bedroom she quickly changed out of her work clothes and into a comfortable pair of stretchy sweatpants and a long sleeved T-shirt, and pulled on her father's old robe over it all. She cinched the sash around her thickening waist and rested her hand on her belly. Now at sixteen weeks, this pregnancy felt different than her last but she was afraid to hope that everything would be okay.

She needed a distraction, she decided as she stroked the fabric of the robe. Maybe now would be as good a time as any to sort out her father's personal papers. Wade didn't seem to be in a hurry for them to go through her father's room. Perhaps she could have it all done by the time he returned.

Piper lit the fire that was set in the grate in her father's suite and drew the drapes to help keep the warmth in. The Dexters had obviously been airing the room on a regular basis because not so much as a trace of his presence remained. It was more than four months since his death and yet sometimes it still felt as raw as if she'd just heard the news.

She settled by the escritoire in the corner of the room and busied herself deciding on what needed to be kept and what should be burned. It was about an hour later that she cast off the robe and pushed up the sleeves of her T-shirt. She must have put too much wood on the fire, she thought as she realized that she had begun to sweat, but hard on the heels of the sweat came another round of chills.

This was ridiculous, she thought, shrugging the robe back on again, this time leaving it open. She was making good headway on her father's papers and didn't want to stop now. She still didn't feel hungry and it wasn't too late yet. She'd just check this one drawer before going back downstairs and heating up dinner.

The drawer contained a flat file box with her name on it. Startled, Piper lifted it out. She had never known her father to express any sentimentality over her childhood certificates and awards, so what could he have in here? She lifted the lid, surprised to see a collection of her old school reports and every single childishly hand-drawn card she'd made for Father's Day or Rex's birthday. Tears filled her eyes as she looked through them. The fact he had kept every one was proof positive that, in his own way, he had cared about her, that she'd mattered to him. She felt the knowledge finally begin healing the gaping hole in her heart. Swiping away the moisture on her cheeks with the cuff of one sleeve, she set the mementos aside and pulled out the plain manila folder that lay at the bottom.

She opened the cover and was surprised to see the logo of a health insurance company. The name jogged her memory. It was the company her father had insured her under when she'd left to go overseas. But what was he doing with all these papers?

She spread them out on the desk surface in front of her. For the most part, they appeared to be a record of premiums and notifications of increases, or decreases, in available benefits. But then two words sprang out at her from a stapled set of papers.

Spontaneous abortion.

Piper's hand shook as she picked up the report and read it more thoroughly. Of course her father would have gotten the wrong end of the stick. Medical terminology had never been his forte. He probably read those two words and didn't read any farther—and then he'd done the unthinkable and told Wade.

She felt sick to her stomach. All that anger, all that sorrow, Wade had borne these past years—all for the sake of a misunderstanding? It just wasn't right. Not only that her father could think her capable of taking a life, but that Wade had believed she had done so, also. Her first instinct was to pick up a phone and call him, to tell him that she had the proof that she was telling the truth, but caution stayed her hand. This was a discussion that was far better held face-to-face.

Piper placed the papers carefully back on the desk and started to sort through the balance of information. A swell of nausea hit her hard, along with it another flush of heat that saw her body bloom with perspiration. She should have stopped to eat. She'd noticed she only suffered nausea with this pregnancy when she didn't eat little bits often. The rest of the papers would have to wait until tomorrow.

She stood and gripped the desk and groaned as a spear of pain shot through her head. The last time she'd felt this bad had been when she'd had malaria. A shock of fear hit her with seismic effect. Could she be suffering a relapse? May had mentioned this could be a serious issue, with treatment being problematic for the baby.

Piper cupped her belly with both hands. No, not again. She didn't want anything to happen to this baby. Hadn't she already borne enough loss in her life? And Wade—he wouldn't believe she hadn't done something on purpose.

She stumbled toward the door. She had to call May, but the doctor's number was in her handbag, which she'd left downstairs. As she stumbled down the first flight of stairs, all she could think of was Wade and how she needed him to know she wanted this baby to be all right, that she'd tried her hardest and that even now she wasn't going to give up. It was on the landing halfway down that she lost her fight for consciousness, the piercing pain in her head too much for her anymore.

Fifteen

"Miss Piper! Miss Piper!"

Dexie's worried voice penetrated the fog of pain and heat that held her body captive.

"Dexter, call an ambulance, quickly. And call Mr. Collins. He left his contact details in the library."

"N-no." Piper struggled to form the words her confused brain knew had to be said. "Don't tell Wade. Not yet."

"Don't fuss yourself, Miss Piper. He needs to know."

"N-not until we know what's wr-rong," she said as a violent shiver shook her body, making her teeth chatter. "D-Dr. Ritter. Her number. It's in my b-bag. Call her. T-tell her… m-malaria."

Her eyes slid shut, speech suddenly too much for her. She felt Dexie's hand repeatedly and gently stroke her forehead, the sensation soothing her as she slid back into unconsciousness.

Two more nights and he'd be home. Things had been chaos when he'd arrived but he was making headway. The most important thing was that none of the exports they'd organized out of the region had been jeopardized and everything remained on track. Now it was just a matter of waiting for Roy to show up and briefing him on what was to happen next.

Wade picked up the glass of brandy he'd ordered from the bar and looked out across the hotel pool and past it to the lagoon. It was an idyllic setting, especially considering the wintry weather he'd left behind him at home, but it wasn't a setting to be enjoyed alone. Maybe he should have brought Piper with him after all. The thought snuck into his head before he could quell it, and with it, brought a surge of longing.

Without stopping to consider what he was doing he reached into his pocket and extracted his cell phone, automatically punching in the numbers to call home. The phone rang several times before the harried voice of Dexter answered.

"Dexter? Is everything okay?" Wade asked.

"Oh, sir. Thank goodness you called. The ambulance has just been here. I was going to call you once we knew where Miss Piper was being taken."

The relief in the older man's voice was palpable, reaching across almost three thousand kilometers and delivering a punch of fear square in Wade's gut.

"What's wrong? What happened? Is she all right?"

Hard on those questions came another. Had she done something to harm the baby?

"We came home this evening to find Miss Piper collapsed on the stairs. We have no idea how long she'd been there in that state. We would have gone straight to our cottage and wouldn't have come in the house if there hadn't been so many lights on inside. Mrs. Dexter was worried. Thank goodness we checked."

"She fell?"

"No, she's ill, sir. The ambulance officers weren't sure

what it was but she kept refusing any medication in case it hurt the baby."

Wade got what details he could from Dexter before leaving his untouched drink on his table and heading back to his room. His frustration mounted as he tried to book a flight home. The soonest he could get on board a plane was at almost 2:00 a.m. He looked at his watch. There had to be another way he could get home faster.

He tried charter companies but in the end it would only have taken longer to get a plane to Apia that he could then travel on to Auckland. The hours until he could get home and make sure that everything—every*one*—he corrected himself, was okay, stretched out interminably.

Staying here at the hotel a moment longer was just going to drive him crazy. If he was out at the airport, he'd feel that he was at least a little closer to heading home. He quickly threw his things in his case and grabbed it and his laptop and headed for the door.

At the airport his frustrations increased a thousand fold as the early hour he'd gone out there meant he couldn't check in yet. But finally he was on the plane and headed in the direction he needed to be going.

His whole focus had been on getting on the next available flight home, but now he was forced by the four-hour flight to stop and wait—and think. Those thoughts immediately turning to the woman who'd never been far from his mind the whole time he'd been away.

Something just didn't gel with what Dexter had said. She'd refused any medication. Her first concern had been for the baby. This wasn't the Piper he thought he'd left behind. She'd been talking about getting rid of their child, just like she'd done before. Refusing medication wasn't the action of woman who didn't have a care toward the life growing within her. It had a lot more to do with a woman who was prepared to protect that life at all costs.

The possibility made him rethink that awful night in the nursery, turning over their conversation in his mind again and again. She'd never actually said she wanted to be rid of the baby and she'd tried to make him believe the loss of their first infant had been out of her control. Even faced with the fact that he knew about that first pregnancy, she'd been adamant—her story not wavering a millimeter.

Had he jumped to conclusions and heard only what he had believed she'd been saying, instead of what she'd meant all along? Had he been wrong about her? A fist clutched in his chest. He wanted to be wrong about her. He'd always wanted to be wrong about her. Finally he allowed himself to face the truth. He'd seen the evidence with his very own eyes. Piper had been different since she'd come home. More settled, more willing to take on responsibility. Going so far, even, to give him the child he'd insisted upon even though the prospect had clearly terrified her.

That took a new level of bravery. Sure, he'd had her between a rock and a hard place over the money and all the things that should rightfully have been hers. But she'd still had the option of walking away. Granted, *with* nothing and probably *to* nothing, but a woman who had as much pride as Piper had always had, wouldn't have thought twice about turning her back on the debt. Somehow she would have found a way to survive.

Survive. Hard on that thought came a deeper concern. If Piper was ill, it had to be pretty serious for her to collapse as she had. And it was with that thought that Wade knew that he didn't want anything to happen to her—ever. He loved her, and he hoped against hope that he would have the chance to tell her face-to-face. To tell her that he was sorry for all the pain he'd put her through, and to beg her forgiveness.

It was 5:00 a.m. in Auckland when the plane touched down. Wade disembarked as swiftly as he could and processed through immigration before the interminable wait at the baggage claim. He considered just leaving his suitcase on the carousel, and sending for it later, but even as the thought formed in his mind his Louis Vuitton case appeared. He scooped it up and headed for customs, thankfully without issue, and headed straight for the taxi line outside the terminal building—one thing and one thing only on his mind. Piper.

The sun was rising as the cab pulled up outside Auckland City Hospital. Wade could only hope that the feeble rays punching through the dark clouds were a sign that everything would be okay.

May Ritter was at the nurses' station when he arrived on the floor Piper had been admitted to. She turned at the sound of his feet marching at a fast clip on the vinyl floor.

"Wade, you got here fast. What did you do, charter a plane?"

"I couldn't, or I'd have been here sooner. How is she?"

"We've stabilized Piper's fever and fetal monitoring shows everything is normal."

"Thank God. A fever? Why? What's wrong with Piper?"

May smiled and laid a hand on his arm to reassure him. "It's a particularly nasty strain of one of the current influenza viruses. It was a relief to us all that it wasn't a relapse of malaria, the symptoms presented very similarly, and Piper told me that it was her biggest fear."

"Her biggest fear, why?"

"She'd contracted malaria a while back, during her volunteer stint abroad. I believe she was working at a women's clinic in Africa at the time—it was the first of several tours she did with various agencies through many countries. It's hard work and can be soul destroying, but she stuck it out despite getting sick. Did she never tell you that?"

"No, I didn't even know she'd done volunteer work."

Wade shook his head in disbelief. Piper? Volunteering to help those far less privileged? It didn't fit with the girl who'd left him, but for some reason it seemed to suit the woman who'd returned.

"Apparently she's been all over the place. Mostly Africa and Asia. You'll have to get her to tell you about it some time."

"Yes, yes, I will," he said, admitting to himself that there was a whole other side of Piper that he needed to know and understand. "Can I see her?"

"She's resting."

"I won't disturb her, I just want to see she's okay."

"Sure, I can understand that. But don't wake her. Her fever's down and she needs the rest more now than anything. All going well, we might even be able to let her home later today."

"Don't rush her out. If this is the best place for her I don't give a damn what it costs, keep her where she'll get the best care."

"We won't let her out until she's ready, but I think she'll be fine. Usually when a flu case presents like this we'd be administering medication, but there doesn't appear to be any problems with the baby and Piper has expressed a wish that we hold off unless absolutely necessary. Bearing her wishes in mind, however, you can rest assured that if her illness presented any issues for the baby we'd be treating her."

"Thank you," Wade said, feeling relief begin to ease the tension in his shoulders and neck. "Where is she?"

May indicated the room two doors down from the nurses' station and issued a final warning not to disturb her patient.

"Don't worry," Wade said, "I want her to be well again, too."

He felt his heart hitch in his chest as he pushed open the door and entered Piper's room. The lighting had been subdued and she looked very small and alone in the hospital bed. He left his cases just inside the door and crossed to the chair next to the bed, lowering himself quietly into it. He scanned her face, noting the sweep of her lashes on cheeks stained with a faint flush of fever. She appeared to be sleeping normally and he felt himself relax by degrees, sinking back into the chair to watch the steady rise and fall of her chest.

He had no idea what time it was when he saw her move beneath the covers.

"Wade?"

Her voice made him sit upright. "Shall I call the nurse? Are you okay?"

"I didn't do it on purpose, you have to believe me," she said, her voice a weak whisper as she drifted back to sleep again.

Her words sliced through to his heart. He'd been such an ogre that her first thought on waking was to defend herself to him. It was no better than he deserved. He'd made such a total hash of all of this. He'd treated her with a complete lack of respect, thinking only of his own agenda and hoarding his bitterness over the past close to him—allowing it to color his every decision. And why? All because he still allowed his father's choices and decisions to sway his own direction.

He'd long since become his own man. Why did he let his old man's abandonment drive him even now? He was a success in business, something his father had never achieved. He had wealth and position in society, again things Eric Collins had failed at. And Wade had the chance to make something good out of something bad, instead of walking away from it and never looking back—so what was holding him in the past?

He knew what it was like to stand on his own, to fight for everything that came his way and create opportunities for those things that didn't. Had it really been so different for Piper when she'd left home? She'd been on her own, completely alone. Could he continue to blame her for decisions she made back then? Things he'd had no knowledge of, things he couldn't change now even if he'd had.

The icy grip around his heart began to soften and melt as

Wade realized that no matter what she'd done before, what mattered most to him was her well-being. Now and in the future. And he wanted to be a part of her future. He wanted to love her and protect her and stand beside her through the next stage of their lives, together.

But would she let him? Would she ever believe that he forgave her for not telling him about their first baby? Would she ever let him love her again?

Wade sat motionless in the chair at her bedside for several hours. Just watching her sleep. It was around lunchtime that May returned to check on her patient and ordered him home to get some rest. He eventually agreed, but only on the proviso that the hospital contact him the moment Piper woke. Piper's fever had returned and it was unlikely she'd be coming home today. The knowledge that she and their baby were still at risk struck fear into his heart. He wanted her to be well again so he could begin repairing the damage he'd wrought.

The cab ride home passed in a blur. He'd been on the go now for more hours than he could count. When he got home he updated the Dexters on Piper's progress and then made his way wearily upstairs. As he reached the door to his suite, he remembered that Mrs. Dexter had mentioned that last night, Piper had been in her father's old rooms.

Had she started packing up in there? he wondered. He dropped his cases inside his sitting room and walked along the landing toward Rex's room and flicked on the lights. Nothing much seemed to have changed in here, although there was a scatter of papers on the escritoire that hadn't been there before. He crossed the room and sat down, turning on the brass lamp which cast a pool of light over the papers.

He thumbed through them, quickly identifying them for what they were. He went to tidy them into a neat stack and put them back inside the file box they'd obviously been taken from when one word leaped out from the page— "abortion."

The bitter taste of regret rose in his throat. He had to learn to put this behind him, he just had to. He'd forgiven Piper already, in his heart and in his mind, but some perverse desire to know all the details saw him select the papers from the stack and sit down to read them carefully. The more he read, the more bitter the taste grew in his mouth.

Spontaneous abortion. The medical term for miscarriage, just as Piper had said.

All those wasted years of anger echoed in the room around him. Rex had misread the information from the very beginning. He'd failed to see one very vital point in the report, that the terminology said the loss of the fetus had been spontaneous. One of those tragic quirks of nature that no one could explain.

Wade leaned back in the chair and let the ramifications of what he'd just learned wash over him. No wonder she'd been so reluctant to do what he'd asked of her—asked? Hell, he'd demanded, and he'd demanded knowing that she was in no position to turn him down. He'd taken advantage of her grief over her father's death and her shock at learning of the abysmal position Rex had left her in, and he'd used both to his selfish advantage. And all of it based on a vow he'd made to himself over her perceived betrayal of the child they'd made together.

Wade made a sound of disgust at his own behavior. For so long he'd been solely focused on this one thing. On making her pay for the wrongdoing he believed she'd actively decided upon, and all along he'd been holding her responsible for something she'd had no control over. Something she'd had to endure all on her own.

The thought of her having to face what had to have been a deep personal loss, so far from home, brought a new level of admiration for her. She'd moved on from that, moved forward with her life—apparently devoting it to good deeds, if May were to be believed, and he had no reason not to believe her.

He had no reason not to have believed Piper, either, when

she'd tried to explain her anxieties to him two weeks ago. She would have been at about the same stage of her pregnancy as she'd been when she'd lost their first baby. No wonder she'd begun to doubt her ability to bring the baby to term. Such a fear would only be natural, and she'd had to face it on her own, as she'd faced so much of her entire life. In his unique way, Rex had been an absentee father almost as much as Wade's father had been.

Wade refiled the papers into their folder and placed them back in the box on the desktop. She wouldn't be alone anymore. Not ever, if he had any say in the matter—if she let him have any say, that is.

Piper sat on the edge of her hospital bed and tried to quell the nerves that twisted her stomach. Had she imagined Wade had been here yesterday? He was supposed to still be in Apia until late Monday night. She must have been dreaming. The fever that had racked her body had made everything feel as if the past couple days had happened in some crazy dream sequence.

She laid a hand against her belly, feeling the baby flutter against her hand. As long as the baby was all right, that was the most important thing. May had assured her everything was fine, even going so far as to bring a portable ultrasound to Piper's room to prove that the baby was still okay.

And now she knew the sex of the new life growing so healthily inside her. A little girl. She wondered how Wade would take the news. He had always struck her as the kind of man who'd want a son to carry on the legacy he had built with such pride. A sound at the door made her look up. As if her thoughts had conjured him, Wade stood there looking uncharacteristically unsure of himself.

"All ready to come home?" he asked.

Piper fought to hide her surprise at seeing him here. Maybe

she hadn't imagined his visit last night after all. "I...I thought you were still in Samoa."

"I came as soon as I heard you were ill. The Dexters send their love, by the way. They can't wait to get you home and spoil you."

And you? Piper asked silently. *What about you?* She dragged in a steadying breath. He'd made his feelings clear before he'd left for Samoa; she'd be crazy to expect that to have changed.

"So? Are you ready?" he asked again.

"Pretty much. I'm just waiting for the nurse to bring my discharge papers. Shouldn't be too long."

"Okay," he said, and leaned against the wall behind him, his hands shoved into the pockets of his jeans.

The silence stretched out between them. If they'd been a normal couple he'd be sitting on this bed with her, she thought, rather than maintaining casual sentry duty on the opposite side of the room.

"Wade?"

"Piper—"

"You first," she said.

"No, it's okay. What I have to say can wait. Probably best said at home, anyway."

She felt a clutch of fear grip her throat. What was it that he couldn't say right here, right now? Did he somehow hold her responsible for what had happened on Friday night? It was a particularly bad case of the flu. Surely he didn't hold her accountable for that.

"What did you want to say to me?" he urged gently, distracting her from her thoughts.

"I learned the sex of the baby this morning. Do you want to know?"

He took his hands from his pockets and pushed himself upright. "Know? Of course I want to know."

"It's a little girl."

She watched as a variety of expressions chased across his handsome features. Disbelief followed by a sheer joy that lit his eyes and made them shine like highly polished steel.

"A girl? That's amazing. Me, us, having a daughter."

"Well, it was always going to be one or the other," she said with a wistful smile.

Either way it made no difference. He didn't want her to be a part of their baby's upbringing. He'd made that patently clear.

"I don't know why but I always assumed it'd be a boy." He paced the room. "A daughter." The words held a note of complete disbelief.

"Are you okay with that?" she asked, feeling a heartfelt surge of protection for her baby. Surely he'd want a daughter just as much.

"Oh, I'm more than okay with that." He beamed. "I never thought I'd be so lucky. Thank you for telling me."

And there it was again, that stiltedness he'd exhibited when he'd come through the door. She felt a tug of sorrow that things couldn't be different between them, that they couldn't have shared this news with the mutual affection and excitement that a normal couple would have.

The nurse arrived at that moment with Piper's discharge papers and a wheelchair.

"I won't be needing that," she protested.

"Yes, she will," Wade amended firmly.

Piper flung him an irritated look. "I'm perfectly fine."

"Humor me," he asked, sending her a look she couldn't quite interpret. "Besides, you're probably not as strong as you think you are. You've been pretty ill these past couple days."

She gave in and settled herself in the chair, surprised by his consideration and, frankly, suddenly too tired to argue. He was, no doubt, quite right in his assertion that she wasn't as fit as she should be. Or maybe it was just this sensation of being on constant tenterhooks around him that made her suddenly feel so weak and incapable.

The ride home was completed in near silence, broken only by Wade asking every ten minutes if she was still comfortable. Once home, she gave herself over to the inevitable fussing from Mrs. Dexter. Finally, though, she was alone in her old room again, propped up against a sea of cushions and with a selection of magazines and a water bottle within easy reach.

Wade came into the bedroom and pushed the door closed behind him.

"Comfortable?"

"I'm fine, thanks."

If he asked her one more time if she was okay, she'd probably scream.

"Are you up for a bit of conversation?"

She stiffened. Here it came. The recriminations for not looking after herself properly, the accusation she'd put another baby at risk. Piper took a deep breath ready to defend herself.

"Bring it on," she said defensively.

"May I?" he gestured to the side of the bed and sat down at her nod.

For several very long seconds he stared at the floor and said nothing but then he turned to face her. She'd never seen him look quite this earnest or vulnerable before. It was a side of him that unsettled her, made her anxious about what it was that he had to say.

"I owe you an apology. Several apologies, actually."

Whatever she'd been expecting from him, it certainly wasn't that. Surprise rendered her dumb. He reached across the covers and took one of her hands in his, his thumb absently brushing back and forth across her inner wrist.

"I have treated you badly, Piper, and I am so dreadfully sorry. I have nothing to say in my defense aside from the fact that I've been a stubborn fool, but I ask that you consider if one day you can forgive me.

"I've always been a driven person, but one who was prepared to work hard to get where they wanted to be. You know a bit about my father and my background, how he abandoned me and surrendered me to the state rather than face up to his responsibilities. I always swore I'd never be like him, that I'd give any child of mine my abiding love and support without question. It's why I was so angry when I heard about your miscarriage."

At her startled gasp he looked up and met her eyes. "Yes, I know it was a miscarriage. I'm very sorry you had to go through that all alone, Piper. I know we can't turn back the clock but I really wish I'd known so I could have been there with you."

"How did you find out?" she finally managed to say.

"I saw the papers you were going through in Rex's rooms when I came back from the hospital yesterday."

"You *were* there," she whispered.

"Yes, and I'd have been there longer if May had let me. I wanted to tell you that I'd forgiven you for what I thought you'd done. That I could understand that, on your own as you were, you probably felt as if you'd had no other choice." His fingers wrapped around hers more firmly, giving her hand a squeeze. "But I was wrong about that as I was wrong about so many things. If I had the chance again, please believe that I'd do it all very differently."

"As you said, we can't turn back time," she said sadly.

"No, we can't. But we can go forward, and I'd really like to go forward with you, Piper. If you'll let me. I'll understand if you don't want to, if you don't want me, God alone knows I deserve worse, but can I ask you to at least consider staying here with me and raising our daughter together, as a proper family?"

"As a proper family?" What exactly did he mean? Did she dare begin to hope?

"I love you, Piper. More than I ever did before and more

than I ever believed I could possibly feel for another human being. I beg of you, please give me another chance. Let me make it right with you this time around. Let me be the man to love you and protect you and stand by you every day for the rest of our lives."

"Wade—" Emotion swamped her, making her eyes tear up and her voice tremble. "I don't deserve this."

"You deserve more, trust me."

"When I was younger, I always thought I loved you as much as one person was capable of loving another, but I know now that those feelings were nothing compared to how I feel about you now. I was too young and immature to understand what I was asking of you when I demanded you come away with me. All I wanted was the reassurance that I came first with you. All my life I'd been second string to my father's work. Nothing I ever did was good enough to get his attention for more than five minutes. I know he loved me in his own way, but it was never enough for me. It made me push so hard for what I wanted that, in the end, I pushed it all away."

She reached out one hand to cup his face. "I didn't deserve your love back then, Wade, but I would like to have another chance to prove to you that I'm worthy of it, of you, now."

"You're more than worthy," he protested before turning his head to place a kiss in the palm of her hand. "I let you down. I didn't understand how much you needed me then. I had my life compartmentalized, my plan ahead of me. You totally upset that apple cart and I didn't know how to do what I wanted to do and keep you at the same time."

"We were both too young to understand it then. I think what I always craved, more than anything, was the reassurance that I was good enough. But I never realized until a few years ago that that acceptance had to come from within me. I've learned that now. I understand that my behavior toward you and Dad was dreadful, but if you can forgive me that, then yes, I would like to be a family with you and our daughter.

"I love you, Wade, more than I ever did before. I want to prove to you that I'm grown up now and worthy of your love, that I'm someone you can rely on in any circumstances, and that I can be a good mother to our children."

Wade leaned forward to brush away the tears she didn't even realize she was crying.

"I know I can rely upon you, Piper. We've both made some pretty terrible mistakes, but at least we've had the courage to learn from them. Will you marry me? Will you be my wife and help me steer a true course for the rest of my life? And then maybe we can keep growing up together?"

"Yes, I will. I'd be honored to be your wife."

"Then there's one place you really need to be," Wade said as he stood and pulled her bed covers aside.

"Where's that?" Piper said, laughing softly.

"With me," he said simply, scooping her up into his arms and taking her to his suite.

And she knew as he placed her gently in their bed and then gathered her in his arms to hold her close that she'd always be number one in his life. Always.

* * * * *

COMING NEXT MONTH

Available November 8, 2011

#2119 WANTED BY HER LOST LOVE
Maya Banks
Pregnancy & Passion

#2120 TEMPTATION
Brenda Jackson
Texas Cattleman's Club: The Showdown

#2121 NOTHING SHORT OF PERFECT
Day Leclaire
Billionaires and Babies

#2122 RECLAIMING HIS PREGNANT WIDOW
Tessa Radley

#2123 IMPROPERLY WED
Anna DePalo

#2124 THE PRICE OF HONOR
Emilie Rose

You can find more information on upcoming
Harlequin® titles, free excerpts and more at
www.HarlequinInsideRomance.com.

REQUEST YOUR FREE BOOKS!
2 FREE NOVELS PLUS 2 FREE GIFTS!

Harlequin®

Desire

ALWAYS POWERFUL, PASSIONATE AND PROVOCATIVE

Harlequin® Special Edition® is thrilled to present a new installment in USA TODAY *bestselling author RaeAnne Thayne's reader-favorite miniseries,* THE COWBOYS OF COLD CREEK.

Join the excitement as we meet the Bowmans—four siblings who lost their parents but keep family ties alive in Pine Gulch. First up is Trace. Only two things get under this rugged lawman's skin: beautiful women and secrets. And in Rebecca Parsons, he finds both!

Read on for a sneak peek of CHRISTMAS IN COLD CREEK. *Available November 2011 from Harlequin® Special Edition®.*

On impulse, he unfolded himself from the bar stool. "Need a hand?"

"Thank you! I…" She lifted her gaze from the floor to his jeans and then raised her eyes. When she identified him her hazel eyes turned from grateful to unfriendly and cold, as if he'd somehow thrown the broken glasses at her head.

He also thought he saw a glimmer of panic in those interesting depths, which instantly stirred his curiosity like cream swirling through coffee.

"I've got it, Officer. Thank you." Her voice was several degrees colder than the whirl of sleet outside the windows.

Despite her protests, he knelt down beside her and began to pick up shards of broken glass. "No problem. Those trays can be slippery."

This close, he picked up the scent of her, something fresh and flowery that made him think of a mountain meadow on a July afternoon. She had a soft, lush mouth and for one brief, insane moment, he wanted to push aside that stray lock of hair slipping from her ponytail and taste her. Apparently he needed to spend a lot less time working and a great deal *more* time recreating with the opposite sex if he could have sudden random fantasies about a woman he wasn't even inclined to like, pretty or not.

"I'm Trace Bowman. You must be new in town."

She didn't answer immediately and he could almost see the wheels turning in her head. Why the hesitancy? And why that little hint of unease he could see clouding the edge of her gaze? His presence was obviously making her uncomfortable and Trace couldn't help wondering why.

"Yes. We've been here a few weeks."

"Well, I'm just up the road about four lots, in the white house with the cedar shake roof, if you or your daughter need anything." He smiled at her as he picked up the last shard of glass and set it on her tray.

Definitely a story there, he thought as she hurried away. He just might need to dig a little into her background to find out why someone with fine clothes and nice jewelry, and who so obviously didn't have experience as a waitress, would be here slinging hash at The Gulch. Was she running away from someone? A bad marriage?

So...Rebecca Parsons. Not Becky. An intriguing woman. It had been a long time since one of those had crossed his path here in Pine Gulch.

Trace won't rest until he finds out Rebecca's secret, but will he still have that same attraction to her once he does? Find out in CHRISTMAS IN COLD CREEK. Available November 2011 from Harlequin® Special Edition®.

HSEEXP1111